40R

THE TRELEON EMERALDS

They all piled into the car

THE TRELEON EMERALDS

by
YVONNE J. CURRY

Illustrated by D. L. Mays

THOMAS NELSON AND SONS LTD
LONDON EDINBURGH PARIS MELBOURNE JOHANNESBURG
TORONTO AND NEW YORK

THOMAS NELSON AND SONS LTD

Parkside Works Edinburgh 9
36 Park Street London W1
117 Latrobe Street Melbourne C1

302–304 Barclays Bank Building
Commissioner and Kruis Streets
Johannesburg

THOMAS NELSON AND SONS (CANADA) LTD
91–93 Wellington Street West   Toronto 1

THOMAS NELSON AND SONS
18 East 41st Street New York 17, N.Y.

SOCIÉTÉ FRANÇAISE D'ÉDITIONS NELSON
97 rue Monge Paris 5

———

LIST OF ILLUSTRATIONS

CHAPTER 1

'PHLIFFELHEIMER,' said Christiane thought-fully, holding her pencil poised above the page of her exercise-book. 'Or would Phloffelheimer be better, do you think?'

'Phliffelheimer,' said Ludovic absently; then, 'Christiane—whatever are you doing?'

'Writing an essay,' said Christiane. 'I was trying to think of a name for the villain.'

'Phloffelheimer then,' said Ludovic. 'Phliffel-heimer is rather frivolous.'

'He *was* rather frivolous,' said Christiane. She wrote down 'Phloffelheimer', scrawled a few lines after it and paused again.

'Ludovic,' she said, 'I can't possibly write an essay at the moment. What's going to happen to us now?'

Her twin brother, Sylvester, looked up from the book he was reading, and for the first time took part in the conversation.

'Let's emigrate to somewhere and call ourselves Tom, Dick and Harriet,' he suggested. Christiane giggled. It was a trial to all of them that both their mother and their father had had a taste for unusual names, with the result that they had called their children Ludovic Montgomery, Sylvester Lancelot and Christiane Marianne Hermione. Ludovic looked down his nose and spoke with mock severity.

'I don't think either of you really care,' he said.

'Well,' said Christiane, 'I don't see why we should. After all, although we live in his great beastly ancestral house, and suffer all the draughts and leaks, and sightseers at half a crown a time, he never came to see us, and never wrote to us, and from all accounts he was rather a horrid old man anyway.'

'Poor Uncle Bob!' said Sylvester. 'The only thing I envy him is his name. I wish he'd left it to me in his will. But what *is* going to happen to us, Ludovic? What did the lawyers say?'

Ludovic was silent for a minute. The interview that he had had that morning with the late Sir Robert Armitage's lawyers had been rather unnerving. Apparently there was nothing but his baronetcy and his house that he had to leave, and both of those naturally reverted to Ludovic, as his heir and the last of his name. There was no money.

Christiane looked at him, and then bent her head over her exercise-book again.

'Isn't there anything?' she asked.

'Nothing at all,' said Ludovic.

'Then it's obvious what we'll have to do,' said Christiane resolutely. 'We must sell this barracks, and all the horses and dogs and stuff, and take just what we need and go and live in Grandma's cottage.'

'Christiane!' said Ludovic. 'What a—a——'

'I think it's a very good idea,' said Sylvester. 'We can't live here, and if we don't sell it, it'll go on being a charge on us.'

'We can't sell it,' said Ludovic flatly. 'It's been in the family for years.'

'No reason why it shouldn't go out,' said Sylvester. 'No-one lives in a house this size nowadays. They can't afford to.'

Ludovic looked helplessly at him. What Sylvester said was true, of course, but he did not want to sell the house. Stanway had been the home of the Armitage family for centuries, and no member of that family would have dreamed, before this, of selling it and living in a cottage. Ever since he had been a small boy, and his parents had been killed in a flying accident, Ludovic had looked forward to the day when he would be Sir Ludovic Armitage and own Stanway. He could think of so many things that could be done to make the place pay again. What he had always dreaded, however, was just what had happened now. Sir Robert had died when his heir was barely twenty-one, had left the house in a shocking state and the estate in a worse one, and landed Ludovic with the care of both the estate and the twins, who were still bound to go to school, being only fourteen, even though there was no money to pay for it. It could only have been worse if it had happened while Ludovic was doing his National Service in the Navy; it was quite bad enough as it was.

Sir Robert had been a rich man at one time, but bad luck and a natural thriftlessness had soon turned him into a very poor man. But he had been used to living well, and nothing would persuade him to give up his horses or his dogs, though he sold his pictures and other heirlooms; but he would not sell his home, or even shut down one wing of the house so that it was less expensive to run. His servants wore themselves out keeping the place habitable, the expense was terrific, and in the end the house had to be thrown open to the public, who could visit it every day but Sunday, in the summertime, for the trifling outlay of two and sixpence for adults and a shilling for children. After that Sir Robert never went near his home, and his nephews and niece had to grin and bear it. And now Sir Robert was dead. There were plenty of debts and no money—but there *was* the house. There was also their mother's mother's cottage in Cornwall, which none of them had ever seen, and which belonged to Ludovic, although he had nearly forgotten about it.

'I'll have to speak to the lawyers,' said Ludovic. 'Anyway, selling the house wouldn't help us all that much, Sylvester. The money we get from that won't last for ever. We'd have to get some more from somewhere.'

'Rob a bank,' suggested Christiane. 'But seriously, Ludovic, if we went to Cornwall you could be a fisherman, or a farm labourer, or something.'

'And who would do the housekeeping and the cooking and the cleaning and the washing and everything?' asked Ludovic. 'We wouldn't be able to afford any help.'

'I expect I might manage,' said Christiane doubtfully.

'And when you were at school?' said Ludovic.

'It need only be a day-school, like we go to now,' said Christiane. 'We could all help in the house, and take turns or something.'

'We'll see,' said Ludovic. 'It might be possible. Anyway, there's no harm in going down to have a look at the cottage, I suppose.'

'When will we go?' asked Christiane immediately.

'Not so fast,' said Ludovic. 'I didn't say we were all going.'

'Of course we will,' said Christiane. 'We wouldn't be able to decide properly if we didn't.'

4

'Hotel bills for three instead of one,' said Ludovic.

'Silly,' said Christiane. 'We can take rugs and things and sleep at the cottage. It'll only be for just one night.'

'And we can take some wood for a fire,' said Sylvester.

'And sausages,' suggested Christiane. 'And bread, and butter, and jam, and——'

'Plates and things,' said Sylvester, 'and something to drink in case the water's turned off.'

'Be quiet, you two,' said Ludovic. 'I'm trying to think. Not that it's not a good idea though . . .'

'We win the first round,' said Christiane gleefully. 'We'll be living there yet. When do we go?'

CHAPTER 2

GRANDMOTHER's cottage was part of a village called Treleon on the north coast of Cornwall. The village boasted a tiny harbour, and a bay for surfing, about three shops including the post office, and an inn, the *Fishing Smack*.

The cottage was small, with a thatched roof and whitewashed walls, and, being the end one of a row, had a good-sized garden, rather neglected. The other cottages in the row were all more or less the same, and yet all different. Some of them, like Grandmother's, were bungalows, some had two storeys. They were all colour-washed, some yellow, but most of them white. One of them was pink.

The Armitages drove into Treleon in the evening, when all the fishermen had congregated outside the inn for a pint and a chat. There was a sudden cessation of talk as the car passed, and everyone turned to watch it out of sight.

' Visitors, likely,' said one old fisherman, and the talk was resumed again.

Ludovic stopped the car outside the cottage and sat still, staring. The twins, squashed into the front seat beside him, also stared, but for a different reason. Ludovic was thinking that the cottage wouldn't be any the worse for paint and whitewash, and someone to weed the garden; the twins were thinking that they were most certainly coming to live here, even if they had to hypnotise Ludovic to make him agree. For one thing the cottage, although dirty, was lovely; for another the harbour was so near; for another there would be swimming

6

in the sea; and for another there was a field behind the cottage, where they might be able to keep Butter and Scotch, their two ponies, referred to collectively as Butterscotch.

'Ludovic,' said Christiane, 'look—a field.'

'What of it?' asked Ludovic, who knew perfectly well what she was thinking.

'Butterscotch,' said Sylvester cryptically.

'Fudge,' said Ludovic obscurely, but with deep meaning in the tone of his voice. 'I thought the idea was to sell the horses.'

'We might get enough from the house not to have to sell Butterscotch,' suggested Christiane. 'And that field is just providential.'

'I expect it belongs to an old curmudgeon,' said Ludovic hopefully.

'We could find out before we leave,' said Christiane. 'Couldn't we?'

'It would mean staying two nights,' said Ludovic, opening the car door. 'And we've only got one evening's supply of sausages.'

'We can buy some more in the village tomorrow,' said Christiane. 'It'll take us more than a day to decide to stay, anyway.'

'It doesn't take more than an hour to decide if we can live in a house this size,' retorted Ludovic.

'But, Ludovic dear, it isn't only the house,' said Christiane in a wheedling voice. 'There's the harbour, and the field, and we'll have to find out if it would be worth having Butterscotch here.'

'You can start collecting some of that stuff out of the car,' said Ludovic, dodging the issue for the moment. 'I'm going to open the door.' He was looking for the key, in the case containing the

7

sausages, bread, butter, ginger-beer and other necessaries, as he spoke. The twins obediently got out of the car and began hauling rugs off the back seat. They stood at his back as he fitted the key into the lock and fell into the hall on his heels. Christiane wrinkled up her nose.

'Smells musty,' she said. 'And just look at the dust ! We must sweep it.'

'No broom,' said Ludovic unhelpfully.

'I expect we can borrow one next door,' said Christiane. 'Hang these rugs over the rail outside, twin, where they can't collect the dust, and I'll go and ask.'

Ludovic took her rugs from her and took them outside again.

'I suppose you're right,' said Sylvester, following him. 'It *is* a bit dirty.'

Christiane went next door and rang the bell, while her brothers leaned against the car and watched her. They saw, from where they stood, the lace curtains in the window drawn aside and quickly let go again. Almost immediately the door was opened by a thin spinster, very neat and trim, and staring down her nose at Christiane, who was looking rather travel-stained. However, in spite of her unprepossessing exterior, Miss Penrose must have had a kind heart, because she lent Christiane not only a broom, but a duster, a floor-cloth, and a bucket of hot soapy water.

'You'll find no water laid on,' she said. 'No gas either. You may bring your washing-up over here and do it in my kitchen.'

'Thank you,' said Christiane, 'very much indeed.'

8

She met Ludovic at the door, waiting to take some of her luggage from her. Miss Penrose looked him up and down and said:

'Ah, you'll be Mrs Martin's grandson. There's never any mistaking a Treleon of Treleon.' Ludovic looked puzzled, as well he might, never having heard of any Treleons apart from the village of that name.

'Our grandmother had the cottage once,' said Christiane.

'Well, she was a Treleon,' said Miss Penrose. She smiled at them and retreated back into her own hall. Ludovic and Christiane carried all the borrowed things into the cottage, where they found Sylvester opening all the windows.

'Sensible,' said Christiane approvingly. 'Now let's get down to work. I'll sweep, Ludovic can dust, and Sylvester can scrub the floor.'

'Oh, can he?' said Sylvester.

'Come now, Sylvester,' said Ludovic, 'you don't mind doing a little thing like that, surely?'

'You can talk,' retorted Sylvester. 'You've got the best job of all.'

'You can both go outside and argue while I get the worst of the dust out,' said Christiane. 'Go on—scoot!'

Sylvester and Ludovic hurriedly retired into the street, and Christiane went through one of the doors at the back of the hall and found herself in a small room, which contained a very large bed, rather dilapidated, and a great deal of dust. The ceiling was very sloping, and there was a cupboard let into the wall, with a rusty key in the lock. Through the window was a view of a wilderness that might once have been a garden. Christiane barely gave

9

it a glance and began to sweep the ceiling, which, as she soon discovered, was whitewashed. She did the best she could with it and the walls, and began to sweep all the dust off the floor out into the hall. When there was a small wall of dust piled up outside the door, she jumped over it and shouted for her brothers.

The other room at the back of the hall was even smaller, and had nothing in it at all except a cupboard and a tiny fireplace. Christiane peered into the cupboard and immediately withdrew her head again, sneezing. Then she proceeded to sweep again. When the room was more or less clear of dust she swept out the front room, which had not got even a cupboard but was rather larger than the other two rooms. The last door, on the left side of the hall coming in from outside, led into the kitchen, which had a tiled floor instead of a board one, and an enormous, old-fashioned, wood-burning kitchen range, which Christiane looked at in secret horror. There was a very primitive water-closet behind the kitchen, but no bathroom anywhere. Christiane frowned and went out to sweep the hall. Clouds of dust billowed out into the street, and there were little cushions of it on the steps. Christiane looked at them with a jaundiced eye and went back into the kitchen for an old rusty bucket she had noticed there. Into this she squashed all the dust, and then put the whole lot outside the back door. Then she went to see what her brothers were doing.

When they had finished the sweeping, and washed down the paint, they began to carry things in from the car, and dumped them in a heap on the clean hall floor.

'Who's going to sweep where?' said Sylvester, becoming rather mixed up.

'We have swept,' said Christiane. 'Sylvester, your hair is grey!'

'So is yours,' retorted Sylvester. 'Work can't be good for you.'

'I expect Ludovic's is too,' said Christiane. 'Only being so fair it won't show so much.'

'We'd better go into the garden to comb it, suggested Ludovic. 'There's no point in getting dust all over the place again.'

They went out at the back door and spent an active ten minutes combing their hair. To an onlooker they must have looked completely mad. Miss Penrose saw them out of her kitchen window, where she was preparing her supper, and looked first disapproving and then amused. When Christiane came to return the bucket and the broom, she met her with a friendly smile and asked her if she and her brothers would come to supper.

'We've got sausages,' said Christiane, though doubtfully.

'And what are you going to cook them on?' inquired Miss Penrose gently.

'The stove,' said Christiane, 'Oh . . . We haven't brought any wood.'

'You come along here,' said Miss Penrose. 'There's a cold chicken I cooked this morning, and plenty of tomatoes from the Vicar's green-house, and I've a lot of butter and home-made jam.'

It certainly sounded more exciting than raw sausage, Christiane had to admit. She hedged for a moment or two and then allowed herself to be persuaded, and went back to tell Ludovic and

Sylvester that supper would be served next door in about half an hour.

'Good egg!' said Sylvester.

'No,' said Christiane, 'chicken. And the Vicar's tomatoes. And home-made jam.'

'Sounds all right,' admitted Ludovic. 'What's the betting the poor lady has a fit when she finds out our names?'

'She's more likely to get her tongue tied in a knot,' said Christiane. 'But seriously, it was jolly kind of her to ask us.'

'Kind and providential,' said Ludovic. 'I wonder if she could tell us where we can get some wood to do the sausages for breakfast?'

'What about water?' said Sylvester. 'We can't have ginger-beer for breakfast. It would be most unsuitable.'

'There's a pump outside the back door,' said Christiane. 'I noticed it when I put the dust out. Let's go and see if it works.'

The pump did work, very reluctantly, and the water that came out of it was, like everything else, rather dusty.

'It'll settle down,' said Ludovic. 'But we'd better make sure it's drinking-water before we drink it without boiling it first.'

'Let's go inside and settle where we're going to sleep,' suggested Christiane. 'We'd better toss for the bed.'

'It's a double bed,' said Ludovic. 'I'll toss you for it, and if I win I'll share it with Sylvester.'

He brought a halfpenny out of his pocket, and dexterously tossed it.

'Tails,' said Christiane. Sylvester bent down to look at the coin.

'Heads,' he said. 'Hard luck, Christiane.'

'I don't know why,' said Ludovic, 'but we've stuck to our break-teeth names for ages without any abbreviations. Idiotic of us.'

'How would you shorten Sylvester?' asked Christiane doubtfully.

'To Silly,' suggested Ludovic. 'Come on, you two. We'd better make up the beds before supper.'

They went back into the hall and sorted out the rugs and cushions they had brought. Christiane carried hers into the smallest back room, thoughtfully looked at the extremely hard floor and wished that Ludovic had lost the toss. She made her bed up under the window, and went into the next room to see how the boys were doing.

'Hullo,' said Sylvester. 'Ludovic is out in the garden.'

'Why?' asked Christiane, puzzled. 'There isn't much garden to be out in.'

At that moment she caught sight of him, staggering up from the bottom of the garden under the weight of a huge truss of straw.

'Goodness me!' she exclaimed. 'Whatever...?'

'He went down to see what was in that little black shed,' said Sylvester. 'Has he found something?'

'Straw,' said Christiane.

She and Sylvester went to the back door to help Ludovic in with his load.

'What are you doing?' asked Sylvester in astonishment.

'I thought Christiane might find the floor rather hard,' said Ludovic. 'And when I saw all this straw I had a brain-wave. It's quite dry, and it'll be a lot softer than the floor to lie on.'

He dropped it on the floor of Christiane's bed-

room with evident relief, right by the cupboard
door, and Christiane, reflecting that it was as good
a place as any to sleep, and that moving straw
would be bound to make a mess, left it there and
remade her bed on it. When that was done it was
supper-time, and they left the house and went
next door.

Over supper Miss Penrose asked them if they
intended to stay long in Treleon.

'We're coming to live here,' said Christiane.

'Perhaps,' said Ludovic.

'Of course we are,' said Christiane.

It may have been only Christiane's imagination,
but as she spoke a tight look came about Miss
Penrose's mouth, and her eyes became all at once
hard and angry. The next moment, however, she
was smiling again and offering Sylvester another
tomato, in a perfectly pleasant manner.

The Armitages helped Miss Penrose to wash up
after supper before they returned to their own
cottage. Christiane thought that she seemed in
rather a hurry to be rid of them, but decided that
it was only her imagination again.

There had been a very small amount of dry
wood in the shed where the straw was kept, which
had to be preserved for frying the sausages for
breakfast, and this meant that the cottage would be
rather gloomy to stay in, since there was no light
and no possibility of having even a tiny fire to warm
things up a bit. So Ludovic, Sylvester and Christiane went for a stroll down to the harbour when
they left Miss Penrose's. Once there, leaning against
the harbour wall looking down at the boats drawn
up on the shingle, Ludovic broached the subject
which was uppermost in his mind at that moment.

'We can't possibly stay,' he said. 'It's impossible. We'll have to think of something else.'

'Why can't we stay?' asked Christiane.

'Several reasons,' said Ludovic. 'For one thing there's no bathroom.'

'We can bath in the sea,' suggested Sylvester.

'Pretty sticky,' said Ludovic. 'And anyway there's the winter to consider as well as the summer. If you fancy washing under the pump with snow on the ground, I don't.'

'There needn't necessarily be snow,' said Christiane. 'And anyway we could buy a tin bath and boil the water on the stove. It would mean only one bath a week, but we could manage.'

'Then,' said Ludovic, 'there's the laundry.'

'We'd have to get someone in from the village to do that,' said Christiane. 'Say once a fortnight, to keep down the expenses a bit.'

'Even so, what do we pay her with?' asked Ludovic sarcastically.

'Money,' said Sylvester. 'Next, please.'

'No lighting,' said Ludovic.

'Lamps,' said Christiane. 'That's an obvious one.'

'The house needs redecorating before we can live in it,' said Ludovic.

'We can do that ourselves,' said Sylvester. 'It's only a matter of paint and whitewash. No wallpaper or anything. And all the inside woodwork is stained. No painting there, only polishing.'

'We could have fun painting the place ourselves,' said Christiane. 'You'd enjoy it as much as we would.'

'Then,' said Ludovic, 'there is the question of money. We haven't any, you know.'

'We'll get over that later,' said Christiane. 'Go on.'

'More important than anything,' said Ludovic, 'none of us can cook anything—except sausages.'

'We can buy a cookery book,' said Christiane.

'Hmmm!' said Ludovic. 'And then you two want Butterscotch. We'd have to pay rent on the field, I have no doubt, and then there's stabling for the winter, and fodder and so on.'

'We can think about that later,' said Christiane. 'You see, there's no problem really. We can bring what furniture we need from Stanway, and anything else we can buy with what's left over when we've sold the house and bought off all Uncle's creditors.'

'But we've got to live after that,' said Ludovic. 'You *will* keep forgetting that.'

'We'd have to live even if we stayed at Stanway,' Sylvester pointed out. 'And it's much cheaper doing it here than in that great thumping house.'

'You have an answer for everything,' said Ludovic. 'But the point is, twins, if we leave Stanway we'd much better go to a town, where it would be easy for me to get work.'

'But we don't want to go to a town,' said Christiane. 'You don't, either. You know you don't.'

Ludovic didn't answer that, but stared thoughtfully at the still, oily water of the harbour. It was beginning to grow dark, and the wind had dropped so that the harbour was as still as glass. The only moving thing was a small rowing-boat with two children in it, slipping through the water towards them. A voice came clearly to them over the water.

'Okay, Lois: ship your oars now.' The person rowing in the bows shipped her oars with a rattle, and dropped overboard into the shallow water to pull the boat ashore. As she came nearer she was seen to be a girl about Christiane's age, with fair hair cut short and very curly. Her companion was a boy, who was undoubtedly her brother and was, mysteriously, about the same age.

' Twins, I bet,' said Christiane with a chuckle. Her voice, but not her words, reached the two in the boat, and the boy looked up. For a moment he looked straight at them, an odd expression in his eyes; then he turned and collected up the four oars before jumping out on to the shingle. The two of them walked away in the direction of the village, talking in low tones, both of them carrying a pair of oars over their shoulders.

' How queer ! ' said Christiane. ' That boy was just like you, Ludovic ! '

CHAPTER 3

In spite of the straw Christiane spent an uncomfortable and restless night.

The cupboard had not been a good place to put her bed, she soon discovered. There was a draught whistling down her neck, and a smell of damp. Also, the straw went into lumps very soon, and she kept rolling off it and falling on the floor with the rugs tangled round her, so that she had to stand up and remake her bed after every fall. She tried moving the straw, but in the dark this was impossible and only made things worse, but she spread it out a bit, rolled herself in the rugs so that only her topmost curl was showing, and resolutely shut her eyes. About one o'clock in the morning she managed to get off to sleep, but almost immediately she woke up again.

She lay for a quarter of an hour, wishing that she had called ' heads ' instead of ' tails ', and then something horrible happened—at least it seemed horrible at the time. There was the sound of soft footsteps in the room, and a horrid echoing voice called out:

' Treleon ! Treleon ! ' The voice died away on a ghastly choking wail and Christiane leapt to her feet, and with the rugs trailing round her and a cushion clutched to her chest, and a few strands of straw in her hair, rushed into the boys' room, unable to bear it any longer.

Both her brothers were asleep, but as she came in the door Ludovic opened one eye and muttered something that sounded like ' Gerwi '. Christiane dropped her cushion and seized his shoulder, shaking it until he was properly awake.

'Whatever is it?' he asked sleepily.

'There's a ghost in my bedroom,' quavered Christiane. 'Oh, Ludovic—it was beastly!'

'A ghost?' said Ludovic. 'What did it do?'

'It shouted,' said Christiane.

'What did it shout?'

'"Treleon! Treleon!"' said Christiane. 'Then it gave a kind of howl.'

'Sounds like a mare's-nest,' said Ludovic. 'If it was a ghost it would have shouted something to the point. You've been reading too much about "ghoulies and ghosties and long-leggety beasties".'

'I was not dreaming,' insisted Christiane.

At that moment Sylvester rolled over and muttered:

'Lois. A good plain name.' And he suddenly sat up with a start.

'Christiane has seen a ghost,' said Ludovic.

'I didn't see it. I heard it,' said Christiane.

'Same thing,' said Ludovic.

'A ghost?' said Sylvester. 'What did it do?'

'Shouted and howled,' said Ludovic.

'It can't have been a ghost,' said Sylvester. 'There must be a perfectly natural explanation. Nightmares or something.'

'It wasn't nightmares,' said Christiane. 'I don't have them. And I will not go and sleep in that room again.'

'Where do you intend to sleep, then?' inquired Sylvester.

'Here,' said Christiane. 'On the floor.'

'You're welcome,' said Sylvester.

Ludovic began unwinding himself from his rugs.

'You can have the bed,' he said. 'Sylvester and I are going to sleep in the other room. But I bet *I* don't get nightmares, or hear so much as a whisper.'

'You probably won't,' said Christiane. 'It'll have gone by now. Morning's coming.'

They spent the rest of the night in great discomfort next door, but heard no sound and saw nothing. Towards morning Ludovic fell into a bruised and indignant sleep, only to be wakened a couple of hours later by a penetrating smell of burnt sausage. On going into the kitchen to investigate, he found Sylvester looking at three charred sausages in a small frying-pan, and Christiane cutting bread.

'Morning, Ludovic,' said Christiane cheerfully. 'Don't look so worried—the other six are all right. We forgot to bring a frying-pan, and we had to borrow from Miss Penrose. She asked if we'd slept well.'

'And what did you say?' asked Ludovic.

'I said "Yes, thank you",' said Christiane. 'But it wasn't very true, was it?'

'Not in the least true,' Ludovic agreed, and went outside to wash under the pump.

When he came back into the kitchen he found Christiane and Sylvester wondering where to lay breakfast, since there was no table, and although the draining-board did for cutting bread on, it wasn't very suitable for eating on.

'Let's take it into the garden,' said Ludovic. 'Did you remember any plates?' he added, seeing the frying-pan full of sausages on the stove.

'No,' said Christiane. 'We'll have to use fingers. I forgot the knives and forks as well—and the cups. We'll have to drink ginger-beer out of the bottles.'

They carried the frying-pan, the bread, the butter, the marmalade and three bottles of ginger-beer out into the garden, and there, sitting up to their shoulders in long grass, they ate their breakfast. Miss Penrose, seeing them out of her kitchen window, looked as if she wondered if they were mad or just silly. Actually they were enjoying the novelty.

They washed up under the pump, and when that was done went down to the village to see if they could buy plates and knives and forks and cups and more sausages. Then Sylvester and Christiane carried their purchases home while Ludovic went into the *Fishing Smack* to find out who owned the field.

The twins left their burdens in the kitchen and went out into the garden. Over the low wall that separated them from Miss Penrose's garden they could see Miss Penrose herself, pruning roses.

'You know what I think?' said Sylvester in a low voice. 'I don't think I like that person.'

'I don't think she wants us here,' said Christiane. 'I think she'd rather we stayed at Stanway.'

'Don't be silly!' said Sylvester. 'Why should she object to our being here?'

'I don't know,' said Christiane. 'But I'm sure she does. She looks at us sometimes in a sort of way . . . I can't explain it.'

'It's those nightmares again,' said Sylvester. 'I say, Christiane, I'd forgotten until this moment, but I meant to have a look in your cupboard this morning. Let's go and do it now.'

'It's very dark, and full of dust,' said Christiane, who had not the least desire to look into any cupboard, anywhere, after the events of the previous night.

'I thought you'd swept it,' said Sylvester.

'I did,' said Christiane.

'Then it can't be full of dust,' said Sylvester with finality. 'Oh look—the Penrose has seen us. We'd better go and be polite.'

They went over to the garden wall, where Miss Penrose was smiling and waving to them.

She's always smiling, thought Christiane. I *don't* like her one little bit.

'Good-morning, twins,' said Miss Penrose. 'How are you this morning? I was surprised to hear you slept well last night. So primitive, it must have been. Not at all what you've been used to.'

'We slept all right when we did sleep,' said Sylvester. 'My sister had nightmares, though. Thought she heard ghosts.'

'Sylvester!' said Christiane reproachfully.

'Ghosts?' said Miss Penrose, with a pleasant vague smile. 'Do you mind ghosts? Some people don't, you know.'

'We've got two ghosts at home,' said Christiane. 'One walks up and down the dining-room at six o'clock on Wednesdays, and laughs when anyone sees it. But *we* never have—I mean seen it.'

'We don't use the big dining-room now,' said Sylvester, 'so of course we don't see it. But there's another ghost that we've all seen. It walks about the house, and smiles politely and doffs its hat when it meets anyone. Neither of them's very horrible.'

'Oh, really?' said Miss Penrose. 'That's most interesting. And do you intend to stay at the cottage?'

'We haven't decided,' said Christiane. 'We may do.'

'I don't think it would suit you,' said Miss Penrose. 'You're used to towns and things, I have no doubt. There isn't even a picture-house down here.'

'We've only been to a cinema once in our lives,' said Sylvester. 'Mostly we go to the theatre. And we were born and brought up in the country.'

Miss Penrose looked rather taken aback.

'Oh, really?' she repeated, and with another vague smile moved away.

'You offended her rather, Sylvester,' said Christiane.

'Well, I'm not sorry,' he returned. 'Nosy old busy-body! I wonder if Ludovic is back yet?'

Ludovic was not back yet, but he appeared in about half an hour, looking rather gloomy.

'Hullo,' said Christiane. 'What's up?'

'The landlord of the inn owns that field,' said Ludovic. 'He says we're welcome to use it, and he can stable Butterscotch at the inn as well.'

'Then what's the trouble?' asked Christiane.

'*That* is the trouble,' said Ludovic. 'And there's also a shortage of young men in the fishing-fleet, and I could get a job as easy as wink.'

'Then there's nothing to stop us coming here?' said Sylvester.

'Nothing at all,' said Ludovic sadly.

Lunch was more sausages, and after it Sylvester again broached the subject of Christiane's cupboard.

'I don't expect Christiane would object if you wanted to look in her cupboard,' said Ludovic. 'It's empty, anyway.'

'Come and tell us if you find a skeleton,' said Christiane. 'I'm going out in the garden. Coming, Ludovic?'

Sylvester scowled after their retreating backs, and went out into the hall.

'I hope he doesn't find anything,' Christiane confided to Ludovic. 'I think I'd rather it was a headless haunt.'

'It's certainly not that,' responded Ludovic. 'Much more likely to be nightmares, if you ask me.'

They settled down in the garden to a strenuous hunt for flowers among the weeds, to find out what was there and what wasn't. Christiane had just found the prize of the afternoon, a round bed of polyantha roses, when her bedroom window opened with a crash, and Sylvester called out:

'Hi, you two! There *was* something there.'

'A skeleton?' asked Ludovic, interested.

'Not a skeleton,' said Sylvester. 'Come and see.'

Christiane and Ludovic left the garden and went indoors. Sylvester was waiting for them outside the door of Christiane's bedroom. They followed him inside and looked at the cupboard. The door was shut, and it looked like an ordinary cupboard.

Sylvester opened the door, and his brother and sister looked in.

'Just an ordinary cupboard,' said Ludovic.

'With an ordinary inside.' said Christiane.

'You're both wrong,' said Sylvester. 'It's a most extraordinary cupboard.'

He pushed them both out of the way and stepped inside the cupboard.

'See this hole?' he said. Ludovic and Christiane peered into the darkness.

'No,' said Christiane, 'we don't.'

Sylvester took her hand and pushed it against the wood.

' Feel it now ? '

' Yes,' said Christiane. ' Ow ! I've got a splinter.' She withdrew her hand and Sylvester pointed out the hole to Ludovic.

' Feels like a keyhole,' said Ludovic.

' That's what I thought,' said Sylvester. ' But why should there be a keyhole in the back of a cupboard ? '

' False back,' suggested Christiane.

' Obviously,' said Ludovic.

' But what's behind it ? ' said Sylvester.

' A skeleton,' said Ludovic.

' Stop harping on that skeleton,' said Sylvester. ' You're just being silly ! '

' We need a key,' said Christiane hurriedly. ' Then we can find out what's on the other side.'

' Try the key of the cupboard,' suggested Ludovic. Christiane, who was nearest, took it out of the lock and handed it to Sylvester, who was inside the cupboard. He fitted it into the lock and turned it. It turned easily, with a soft click, and the door moved slightly towards him. A blast of damp sea-weedy air blew through the room. Ludovic caught hold of the edge of the cupboard and dragged it farther open. There was darkness on the far side.

' We need a torch,' said Sylvester. His voice echoed hollowly back to them from the darkness.

' Well, we haven't one,' said Ludovic. 'And we can't go in there without one.'

' Let's shut the cupboard and go and buy one, then,' said Christiane.

Ludovic agreed, not too reluctantly, and they shut and locked both the doors. Ludovic pocketed the key, and as they left the house the twins noticed that he was frowning heavily.

'What's up?' asked Christiane. 'You look as blue as a megrim.'

'As a what?' asked Ludovic, diverted for a moment from his troubling thoughts.

'A megrim,' said Christiane. 'I read it in a book.'

'Sounds double Irish,' said Ludovic.

'Which book?' asked Sylvester, but by that time they had reached the post office (which sold everything that the grocery and Ye Olde Gift Shoppe did not—and that included torches).

They all three went in to buy the torch, and came out with three torches instead of one because, as Christiane said, there was no lighting in the cottage and they'd very likely come in useful later on. Ludovic frowned again, and said that they might come in useful at Stanway, but he couldn't see where or when. The twins considered this remark merely frivolous, and ignored it.

When they got back to the cottage they went again into Christiane's bedroom and reopened the cupboard. The same blast of cold air met them, and made Christiane shiver.

'Cold?' asked Ludovic.

'N—no,' said Christiane. 'That was a shiver of anticipation.'

Ludovic switched on his torch and shone it into the hole. It lit up a low sloping roof and a flight of rough-hewn steps.

'Curioser and curioser,' he muttered to himself.

'What is?' demanded Christiane. 'You're standing in the way and *we* can't see a thing.'

Ludovic stepped into the hole, and the twins crowded in after him.

'Steps!' exclaimed Sylvester.

'You don't say!' said Ludovic, and began to pick his way carefully down them. The twins followed. At one point where the steps had completely broken away, they had to jump down several feet to the next sound step.

The steps went on for a long time, and towards the bottom became very slimy and treacherous. The air was like that of a vault. Once Christiane slipped and nearly fell.

'Steady,' said Ludovic. 'Oh,' he added, 'I'm at the bottom.'

The twins stood behind him, breathing rather heavily down his neck. The light of their three torches played on the walls of a small cave, dripping with water. The floor was covered in seaweed.

'All very sinister,' said Ludovic. 'What's that rushing noise?'

They all listened carefully. There was a tinkling watery noise over to their right. Cautiously they picked their way over the floor towards it, and found a deep wide cleft in the rocks at their feet, like a small dike, filled with water, and with a tiny waterfall at its head.

'Like a bath,' said Christiane. 'I say, what fun!'

'What is?' asked Sylvester. 'I suppose there must be a spring in the cliff somewhere,' he added.

'Probably the same one that feeds our pump,' said Ludovic. 'It must run right underground and come out here .... I wonder how it escapes?'

'Runs out to the sea, I expect,' said Christiane uninterestedly. She was tired of the spring. It was rather dull. She swung the beam of her torch away from it and shone it across the left-hand wall. Then suddenly she gave a queer sort of gasp and caught at Ludovic's arm.

'Look . . . . Look there ! '

Sylvester and Ludovic looked where her torch was shining, and saw that part of the wall there was flat, like a blackboard, with letters carved on it, reading:

TRELEON TRELEON

JOHN RICHARD AND

LOUISE

1599

THE TIDE WILL

RISE

'What is it ? ' said Sylvester.

'That's what *it* said,' said Christiane in a breathless whisper: ' " Treleon, Treleon ". But why ? It's a senseless thing to say.'

'*It* said it,' said Ludovic grimly, ' because that's what is written here. Come on, let's go back to the room. It is cold in here.'

'What did you mean ? ' asked Christiane, as they went back towards the steps.

'Nothing,' said Ludovic. ' But we are certainly not coming to live in this cottage.'

There was a note of finality in his voice, and for once the twins were silent.

It took them a long time—heaving and pulling each other up the broken section of steps—to reach the cottage again.

CHAPTER 4

CHRISTIANE was sitting in the library at Stanway, continuing the adventures of the villainous Phloffelheimer in her school English book. So far he had proved a most satisfactory villain, but just at the moment he was being refractory, and refusing to do what she wanted. This was partly because half her attention was on Ludovic, who was certainly not villainous but on the contrary recovering from measles, which was most un-villainous, un-romantic and un-everything else. The only thing it wasn't un- was awkward, and it was most that. She suddenly realised that her thoughts were in a muddle, what with ' uns ' and ' thats ', and hurriedly returned her attention to Phloffelheimer.

While Bert [she wrote; Bert was the hero] *was languishing in the deep dark dungeon, his cruel captor was sneaking into the Palace yard in the guise of a . . .*

In the guise of a what? Who could go into a Palace yard without arousing suspicion ? Soldiers ?—no, they wouldn't sneak. Beggars ?—not allowed. Servants ?—that was it !

. . . in the guise of the Queen's lady-in-waiting. He thought it had been clever of him to think of this disguise [it was even cleverer of me] *and he laughed to himself as he thought of poor Bert Beanstalk. 'Ha ha ! I am safe without him around. He wasn't so smart as he thought he was ! ' But at that very moment Bert Beanstalk was . . .*

29

Where on earth is Sylvester? And there is the telephone. I suppose I'd better go and answer it.

She put down her pencil, but at that moment the telephone stopped ringing, so she picked it up again and went on writing.

. . . Bert Beanstalk was . . .

Well, he was freeing himself somehow, but how? The poor man is all tied up in a sack with yards and yards of rope, and chained to the wall into the bargain. He can't possibly escape. Phloffelheimer is right. He just *can't*. And he won't be in time to prevent the Crown Jewels being stolen, and he'll have to be, or the essay will be too long. Oh dear!

Christiane frantically chewed the end of the pencil, and stared out of the window for inspiration.

Her thoughts wandered. Everything was going so badly! Only six weeks since they had come back from Cornwall, and the whole family was in trouble of one kind or another. First, a whole lot more of Sir Robert's debts had come to light; secondly, a fox had stolen or killed over half the hens; and thirdly, Ludovic had got measles. The last thing was the worst. He had had it much worse than the twins had had it, years and years ago, and what with the debts and one thing and another, he just wasn't recovering. He wasn't measly any more, but he'd grown thinner and lost his appetite, and only that morning Christiane had found four grey hairs in his head. At barely twenty-one, too . . .

At that moment the door opened and Ludovic himself came in. He looked tired—he nearly always did lately. Christiane felt unreasonably cross with Sir Robert for dying. She put down her pencil.

'Ludovic, how on earth can a man escape from an impossible situation ? '

'He can't,' said Ludovic. 'Why ? Has Bert Beanstalk got into one ? '

'Yes,' said Christiane gloomily. 'Who was that on the phone ? '

'Mr Wilson,' said Ludovic, flopping down into an armchair.

'The lawyer ? '

'Yes.'

'Oh,' said Christiane. 'What did he want ? Anything interesting ? '

'You'd be surprised if I told you,' said Ludovic ruminatively.

'Should I ? ' said Christiane. She got up from the table and went to sit on the arm of his chair.

'Ludovic—why don't you . . . ' She paused. He looked up at her with a curious little smile on his face.

'Why don't I . . . ? ' he prompted.

'Why don't you sell the beastly house ? ' said Christiane.

'I'm going to,' said Ludovic calmly. There was a short silence, then:

'Why ? ' asked Christiane. 'You don't want to, do you ? '

'No,' said Ludovic, 'I don't. But if I try and keep it on any longer, I think the strain will kill me. Do you know, Christiane, that we have a fortune totalling to minus ten thousand, three hundred and eighty-four pounds ? '

'All that much ? Goodness ! '

'It's rather awful really,' said Ludovic. 'We'll never pay it off. Not if we stay, that is.'

'What can we get for the house ? ' asked Christiane.

'I've just had an offer of fifteen thousand pounds.'

'And where will we go—Cornwall?'

'I suppose so . . . I don't want to.'

'Why not?' asked Christiane.

'Christiane,' said Ludovic, and paused a moment.

'Yes?' said Christiane.

'Did you mind about that—call it a ghost, although it wasn't?'

'Yes . . . I did, rather,' said Christiane. 'And Miss Penrose too was—well, queer.'

'We won't be very popular when we go to live down there,' said Ludovic, with a rather dreary little laugh.

'What makes you say that?' asked Christiane.

'Oh, lots of things,' said Ludovic.

'Miss Penrose liked us all right until we said we were going to live down there,' said Christiane. Then . . . 'Do you think we were imagining everything?'

'Not everything,' said Ludovic. 'That cottage hadn't been lived in for ages, and yet, did you notice that all the locks were freshly oiled in your room? And the window catch? And there was a little path trodden in the grass. I noticed it when we were looking for the plants.'

'I didn't notice,' said Christiane. 'Perhaps— perhaps we'd do better to stay here.'

'We wouldn't,' said Ludovic.

'No,' said Christiane.

'I don't want to go to Cornwall,' said Ludovic. 'Not in the least—but we will go, all the same.'

'Why?' asked Christiane.

'Obvious reasons, mostly. We can't stay here. We haven't anywhere else to go. We'll go for the summer, anyway. We can think about what to do next after that.'

The door opened and Sylvester came in.

' Hullo,' said Sylvester. ' What are you two looking so serious about ? '

' We've decided to go and live in Cornwall,' said Christiane.

' And to sell the house,' added Ludovic.

Sylvester looked at him queerly, but said nothing. Later, when Ludovic had gone away and Christiane was untangling the difficulties of Bert Beanstalk, he suddenly looked up from his book.

' What's changed Ludovic's mind all of a sudden ? '

' An offer for the house,' said Christiane, without looking up.

' I'm glad,' said Sylvester.

' We're not,' said Christiane.

' Why not ? Just because of the Penrose and all the locks ? ' asked Sylvester.

' Did he tell you too ? ' said Christiane.

' No,' said Sylvester. ' He talks in his sleep just lately—half the things he said he'd never tell us awake, I'm sure.'

' Such as ? ' said Christiane.

' All sorts of things,' said Sylvester. ' He kept on and on, saying he'd never sell Stanway. And he keeps saying, " The tide will rise ".' He paused, and looked at his twin.

' " The tide will rise " ? ' said Christiane. ' But that's . . . '

' Quite so,' said Sylvester. ' I think it's a good idea to go to Cornwall, Christiane. There's something funny about that cottage, and I want to find out what it is.'

33

'Just supposing there is——' said Christiane, '—not that I think there can be—what could be funny about it?'

'Something must be,' said Sylvester. 'You can't blink facts. There are all those oiled locks, and the cave, and someone who shouted "Treleon, Treleon" to scare us away.'

'It might have been a ghost,' said Christiane.

'There aren't such things,' said Sylvester. 'Oh, hullo, Sir Edward.'

Sir Edward swept them a graceful bow, and walked through the book-case into the next room.

'Funny,' said Christiane. 'It must be our imaginations, Sylvester. You and I and Ludovic never see him at the same time. It *must* be imagination.'

'Of course it is,' said Sylvester. '*I* only ever see him when the sun's in my eyes.'

'Dear Sir Edward,' said Christiane. 'It'll be hard leaving him. But Sylvester, quite apart from anything else, I should be very glad to drag Ludovic away from here. He's worrying himself to death, and the measles didn't help. He never used to talk in his sleep before, and our family don't go grey early, and nor did Mummy's.'

'Cornwall should put the oomph back into him,' said Sylvester. 'Don't worry, Christiane. We'll muffle through somehow—although at the moment I can't see quite how.'

'Nor can I,' Christiane sighed, and returned her attention to Bert Beanstalk and Phloffelheimer.

CHAPTER 5

' SAUSAGES again,' said Ludovic plaintively. ' We had them for supper yesterday, Christiane.'

'And for breakfast,' said Christiane. ' But I bought some sausage rolls for lunch—just for a change.'

' We'll be looking like sausages soon,' chimed in Sylvester.

' Bessie and Co laid two eggs last night,' said Christiane, ' and another this morning. That's supper.'

' Not meaning to be ungrateful,' said Ludovic, ' but we'll be looking like eggs, too, soon.'

' That'll be breakfast,' said Christiane flippantly.

' Don't be idiotic,' said Sylvester—obviously rather cross. A two-day diet of sausages was spoiling his temper.

' I'm going to get some kippers for tomorrow's breakfast,' said Christiane soothingly. Both her brothers cheered.

Christiane picked up the bread-knife and cut herself a slice of bread.

' By the way,' she said suddenly, do we want a kitten ? '

' What ? ' said Ludovic.

' A kitten,' said Christiane. ' The landlord of the *Fishing Smack* has three kittens—at least, his cat has. A black one, a tortoise-shell one and a ginger one.'

' Rather a mixed bag,' observed Ludovic. ' Do *you* want a kitten, Christiane ? '

' I wouldn't mind one,' said Christiane cautiously.

35

'You can have one if you want it,' said Ludovic.
'But don't have the ginger one. Black ones are best.'

Christiane turned a beaming smile on him.

'I hoped you'd say we could have one,' she said.
'I saw them yesterday, and they're darlings!
We can go and choose one after we've made the beds.'

'You can count me out of the expedition,' said
Ludovic a trifle shortly 'I'm going to nail up that
door at the back of your cupboard.'

'I'm not altogether sorry,' said Christiane, after
meditating. 'I haven't heard anything more, but
the bare thought of it gives me the creepy-crawlies.'

As soon as the beds were made Ludovic disappeared into Christiane's bedroom with a hammer
and a tin of nails, and Sylvester and Christiane
walked down the road to the inn to choose the
kitten. They stopped by the harbour wall, and
looked at the boats lying pulled up on the beach.

'I'm glad we came,' said Christiane. 'Are you?'

'Very glad,' said Sylvester. 'In spite of the
sausages.'

'Quite apart from anything else,' said Christiane,
'Ludovic is rapidly becoming himself again.'

'He was never anyone else,' pointed out Sylvester
mildly.

'You know what I mean,' said Christiane, still
more mildly. 'But really, Sylvester, if it wasn't for
the measles. I don't think we'd be here now. He
was quite capable of sticking it out at Stanway, and
killing himself trying to make a go of it.'

'That's true,' said Sylvester. 'Actually, I thought
he *would* stay. I never really believed . . . Oh look,
there're those twins again!'

Christiane looked where he pointed and saw the golden-haired Lois and her brother, who, in the company of a large St Bernard, were busy baling out a small rowing-boat. Seen in the light of day they weren't particularly like each other, except in colouring, but the boy was still the image of Ludovic. Christiane, who had been thinking that the likeness had been merely a trick of the uncertain twilight, frowned a little.

'Something bothering you, Christiane?' asked Sylvester.

'I was thinking,' said Christiane. 'Why should that boy *be* so like Ludovic? He's much liker than we are. So is the girl, really.'

'It's only colouring,' said Sylvester. 'I do trust that you're not thinking that we've discovered some dark plot to cheat those two out of their rights by putting us in their place when we were all babies?'

'I suppose it's hardly possible,' said Christiane with regret. 'But wouldn't it be fun if we had?'

'Not particularly,' said Sylvester. 'In fact, I think it might be rather beastly. You don't know but what they might be a lot worse off even than we are.'

'They might—easily,' said Christiane. 'But I don't somehow think they are. I wonder *why* they're so like Ludovic?'

'Go and ask them,' suggested Sylvester. He spoke idly, and had no intention of her following his advice, but to his mingled horror and amusement she immediately left his side and strolled across the sand towards the other twins. Mechanically he followed her, mentally rehearsing speeches of explanation.

The girl Lois had noticed their approach, and stood up, baler in hand, waiting for Christiane to reach her. To Sylvester's infinite relief it was she who spoke first.

'Hullo.' she said. 'You must be our cousins. We heard you were thinking of coming to live here.'

Christiane was rather taken aback, and could only stammer, ' C-cousins ? '

'Yes,' said Lois. 'Your grandmother was our great-aunt. We're second cousins, or something. Our name is Treleon,' she added by way of further explanation. 'I'm Lois, and this is John. We're twins.'

'So're we,' said Sylvester. 'I say—your dog's gone hiking off all across the road. Does it matter ? Won't he be in danger of getting run over ? '

Lois and John glanced towards where their enormous pet was lying peacefully on the crown of the road.

'Can you get a rebate on dog licences ? ' asked John lazily.

'She's not really our dog,' said Lois. 'She belongs to Aunt Margaret.'

'Nothing ever comes along here,' said John. 'She'll be all right.'

'Her puppies sold like hot cakes,' said Lois. 'She's a lazy dog.'

'Greedy too,' said John. 'She has very low tastes in food.'

Christiane and Sylvester stood mute in the face of this onslaught of information. Lois looked slightly downcast.

'There we are,' she said: 'at it again. Daddy always says we're quite repulsive to strangers.'

'We start talking in shifts,' said John. 'Do you ? '

38

'Hullo,' she said. 'You must be our cousins'

'No,' said Christiane in a small lost voice.

'It's a terrible habit,' said Lois. 'By the way—you know our names, but what are yours?'

Christiane looked uncomfortable.

'Horrible,' she said forcefully. It was the turn of Lois and John to look surprised. Sylvester went off into a peal of laughter.

'Don't look so surprised,' he said between laughs. 'Oh, Chris! You are funny!'

Christiane, looking rather hot and bothered, hurriedly repaired her error.

'We're called Sylvester and Christiane,' she said apologetically. 'Our surname is Armitage. And we've a brother called Ludovic—we were wondering, actually, why he was so like you, but if we're cousins that explains it.'

'Christiane,' said Lois. 'That's rather a pretty name. Better than Lois.'

'She can't really grumble,' said John. 'She had a narrow escape from being called Louise.'

'It's a family name,' explained Lois. 'So's John. Luckily Mummy couldn't bear it though, so she and Daddy compromised.'

'We talk too much,' said John suddenly. 'Steady it a bit, twin. None of the local donkeys will have any hind legs left in a few minutes.'

There was an immediate silence, during which a large grey car swept down the street, missed the recumbent Tiny by inches, and drew up with an angry screech of brakes opposite the inn. Lois suddenly turned away and stared pointedly out to sea, while John called, 'Tiny! Come here!' The enormous St Bernard leapt up as if someone had stuck a pin in her, and dashed across the road just as a large fat man, wearing a coat with an astrakhan collar, got out of the car. He stared across in the twins' direction for a minute, and then strode into the inn.

'Has he gone?' asked Lois in a brittle voice. 'I will *not* look at him! Horrid, beastly old beast!'

'Stow it!' said John, acutely conscious of the presence of the other twins. 'He's gone. But there's no need to be so dramatic about it.' He clipped Tiny's lead on to her collar and looped it round the rowing-boat's mooring-rope. Tiny, quite unconcerned, lay down on the sand and went back to sleep.

'Lazy!' said Lois, stirring the inanimate heap of dog with her toe. Tiny opened one weary eye, then, unable to support the effort, closed it again with a heavy sigh.

Christiane tugged at Sylvester's sleeve.

'Kittens,' she said. 'And if we're not back soon, Ludovic will be anxious. We said we wouldn't be long, remember.'

Lois seized on one word.

'Kittens?' she said. 'Oh, are you buying one of the landlord's?'

'Yes,' said Christiane. 'We're just going to, this minute. It's what we came out for, really.'

'Please,' said Lois coaxingly, 'may we come and help?'

'You can come with us if you like,' said Christiane. 'But there won't really be much choice about it. Ludovic likes black ones, and as he's paying for it . . .'

In the end, after some argument, all four of them went over to the inn. The landlord's wife greeted Lois and John like old friends, exclaimed in surprise at seeing them at all, and told Christiane

41

that she and Sylvester were even less alike than the two Treleons. This was perfectly true, since Sylvester had dark hair and Christiane rust-coloured hair, and although they both had grey eyes it was the only thing the same about them.

'I've never seen an identical twin,' said Lois conversationally to Sylvester, as they went into the inn yard to have a look at the three kittens.

'I have,' said Sylvester. 'But I'm glad I'm not one.'

'Yes,' said Lois, 'you'd never know if you were you or the other one, would you?' Sylvester preserved a shattered silence.

The kittens were confined in a straw-filled box, playing hide-and-seek with each other, and hitting each other over the head. The black one was completely hidden, all except for his tail, and the ginger one and the tortoise-shell one were having a stand-up fight.

'Darlings,' murmured Lois sentimentally. She picked up the tortoise-shell one and was promptly bitten by the ginger one.

Christiane was staring fascinated at the ginger kitten. He was the smallest of the three, with big yellow eyes and an inquiring tilt to his small furry head. His ears were pricked up, and there was such an expression of pleased expectancy on his whiskers that Christiane couldn't bear to disappoint him. The black one was rather an Alexander-beetle anyway.

'We'll have the ginger one,' she said immediately. 'Oh, the brute!' she added, as she too fell a victim to her protégé.

'Ginger?' said Sylvester. 'Remember what Ludovic said.'

' He won't mind,' said Christiane. Sylvester, who also thought that Ludovic wouldn't mind, said no more. The tortoise-shell kitten was returned to her brother, and the ginger one was paid for, put in a strong paper bag and carried away from his birth-place into the wide wide world. They took him straight back to the cottage, out of consideration for his kittenly dignity, which appeared to be suffering from being shut up in a bag. Ludovic greeted both the kitten and the Treleon twins abstractedly, and asked Christiane if they had any sticking-plaster, since he had succeeded in hammer-ing a nail into his finger by mistake. While Chris-tiane therefore bound up her brother's wounds, Lois buttered the kitten's feet and gave him a saucer of milk, and generally made him feel at home. Sylvester and John sat on the edge of the kitchen table and watched the kitten licking the butter off its paws. When both Ludovic and the kitten had been dealt with it was eleven o'clock, and so the Treleons stayed for elevenses, were shown all over the cottage, and told briefly about the adventure of the first night they had slept there.

' And was there a cave ? ' asked John, interested.

' Most certainly there was a cave,' said Ludovic.

' And yet . . .' said John, half to himself. ' Mr Swanson swore it couldn't possibly exist.'

CHAPTER 6

THE next week passed without event. Ludovic, who loathed veiled utterances, hammered another three nails into the passage entrance to make quite sure, and Lois divulged the interesting fact that Mr Swanson was the man with the astrakhan collar who made a study of local caves and was writing a book on them, and who lived at Treleon House. Since it was quite obvious that neither she nor John could bear him, none of the Armitages had any desire to make his further acquaintance.

Colonel Treleon, the twins' father, called to see the Armitages one day and carried them off back to tea at his house, which was one of the two-storeyed cottages just outside the village. It wasn't really his house, Lois explained, but they had let Treleon House—to Mr Swanson. The cottage belonged to Aunt Margaret, the owner of Tiny. Since the twins had no mother, this aunt had taken her place and brought up the twins since they were two years old. She was older than the Colonel, with fair hair streaked liberally with grey, and with twinkling blue eyes—a true Treleon, in colouring at least.

At the end of the week Ludovic suddenly decided, over his breakfast sausage, that he could no longer survive without a car, and wondered why on earth he had ever been so idiotic as to sell their other one. Christiane pointed out that it was a very expensive car, and hardly in keeping with their straitened circumstances. Sylvester backed her up, and said they had better get a humbler one. The result of this discussion was that Ludovic, with both sets of twins, piled into the Padstow bus and went off to buy a car—a humble car, even a second-hand car, but something that would hold all five of them and not break down under the strain. I say all five of them, because by this time the Treleons and the Armitages had practically adopted each other.

After a rather hectic morning, touring the various garages in the town, they eventually ran to earth the right sort of car. It was an open tourer, painted what Christiane called 'a vulgar shade of scarlet'. It was not really big enough for five, but they managed to squeeze into it during the trial run, and anyway, as Ludovic said, a larger one would be too expensive to run. They left the car at the garage for a general overhaul, and went to a large hotel and had a very expensive lunch. They returned to Treleon on the bus. Since the bus was rather full of sight-seeing visitors, Sylvester and Christiane found themselves separated from the other three, sitting on the back seat of the bus while the others were in the front.

'Are you still glad we came, Sylvester?' asked Christiane.

'Moderately,' said Sylvester. 'Why, aren't you?'

'Yes, of course,' said Christiane. 'But I don't think Ludovic is. He's getting restless. Doing nothing all day doesn't suit him. Nor does sticking about in the village. Hence the car.'

'Well, we can't do anything about it, can we?'

'No,' said Christiane. 'Sylvester—haven't we any relations we could go and live with?'

'We've no relations at all,' said Sylvester,

45

'except the Treleons, of course, and except for Cousin Lizzie, and she wouldn't have us if she was paid. She doesn't believe in " cluttering the place up with children ".'

'I mentioned it,' said Christiane, 'because Ludovic wanted to stay on in the Navy.'

'Did he ? I never knew.'

'You don't know everything,' said Christiane. 'As a matter of fact I only found out by accident. Cousin Lizzie told me. How *she* found out, goodness alone knows.'

'I suppose he couldn't very well leave us all alone,' said Sylvester.

'He wouldn't,' said Christiane. 'If only we could find some way . . . '

'Some way of what ? '

'Oh, Sylvester—don't be so dense ! Some way of settling us so that Ludovic could go back into the Navy.'

'What way ? '

'I don't know,' said Christiane.

Three days after this conversation took place, Christiane was cooking tomato and bacon for breakfast, while Sylvester cut the bread—very badly. Once again the subject of their talk was Ludovic, who appeared to have got up at six o'clock in the morning, and had subsequently disappeared.

'He'll be back for breakfast,' said Christiane. 'That is, unless he thinks it's sausages again.'

'I'm sick to death of sausage,' said Sylvester. 'By the way—have we got them for lunch ? '

'No,' said Christiane. 'We've got fish-cake things. I bought them at the post office.'

'Beg pardon ? '

'The post office,' repeated Christiane. 'In the grocery department.'

'First time I ever heard that fish were grocery,' said Sylvester sceptically. 'Hey—did I hear the door go?'

'You did,' said Ludovic, appearing in the kitchen doorway at that moment. 'Are the sausages ready yet?'

'Not sausages this morning,' said Sylvester. 'Bacon. And tomato.'

'You were up early this morning,' said Christiane. 'Whatever were you doing?'

'Shrimping,' said Ludovic calmly.

'*Shrimping?*' said Sylvester.

'And prawning,' said Ludovic. 'High tide. Shrimps are in. New moon. Prawns.'

'Quite,' said Sylvester.

'Would you like to explain?' asked Christiane, spooning out tomato on to three plates.

'Greatest pleasure in the world,' said Ludovic. 'When the prawns are around, the men in the fishing-fleet go out after them all along the beach. They sell well to the visitors. This morning I went with them. Tomorrow I'm going out after mackerel in the bay—that is, if you two can manage without me.'

Sylvester shot a swift glance at Christiane, and closed one eye in a wink.

'We can manage,' said Christiane. 'Easily ...'

'That's good,' said Ludovic. 'What are you two doing this morning?'

'Exercising Butterscotch,' said Christiane. 'Like we always do. When we've made the beds and washed up, that is.'

'I'll wash up,' said Ludovic.

47

'You're welcome,' said Christiane. 'But don't break anything—and don't forget the frying-pan.'

Nearly an hour later the twins were busy catching and saddling Butterscotch. Butterscotch by the way was—or should it be were?—a pair of Exmoor greys, and like their owners were twins.

'Where are we going this morning?' asked Christiane. 'Anywhere in particular?'

'I thought we might go in the direction of Treleon House,' suggested Sylvester. 'We haven't seen it yet.'

'How funny,' said Christiane. 'No, I don't mean not having seen it: but *I'd* thought we might go there too.'

There were two ways of getting to Treleon House. One could either go along the road and up a rutty lane (which must have been very bad for the springs of Mr Swanson's grey car), or there was a faint path along the edge of the cliff, where there was no road in sight, and very few houses. Christiane and Sylvester chose to go along the cliff.

'It's funny,' said Christiane suddenly.

'What is?' asked Sylvester, jumping Butter over a small bramble. 'Bert Beanstalk?'

'Nothing to do with him,' said Christiane. 'Lots of things since we came here. We're almost living in a Bert Beanstalk story.'

'Gosh, I hope not!' exclaimed Sylvester, remembering some of the dreadful things that had happened to that hero of many grisly encounters with Phloffelheimer, the German spy.

'It's Mr Swanson,' said Christiane dreamily. 'I say, Sylvester, I wonder if he's a villain?'

'No reason why he should be,' said Sylvester, who was becoming rather out of his depth.

'No reason why he shouldn't, either,' pointed out his twin. 'In fact, I think he'd make an excellent villain. Look at his opportunities. He studies caves, which gives him a wonderful chance for smuggling, and he's living in someone else's house, and from what Lois and John's Aunt Margaret said, some of the things in it are pretty valuable. He could be gradually substituting fakes for all the old masters, and no-one need ever find out that he's doing it.'

'*And* he's beastly,' said Sylvester. 'Lois can't stand the sight of him. But that doesn't mean anything.'

'But it *is* funny,' said Christiane.

'What is ?' asked Sylvester for the second time.

'A lot of things,' said Christiane. 'My ghost, for instance, and what John said about Mr Swanson saying the cave didn't exist. You know what, Sylvester ?'

'What ?'

'I think we ought to go into it more thoroughly. I'm sure there's something fishy going on.'

'There's Miss Penrose too,' said Sylvester, catching the spirit of the thing. 'She's been jolly queer about us, and didn't want us to come and live here. She did her best to put us off, if you remember.'

'Of course she did,' said Christiane. 'I'd almost forgotten that. I expect she's hand in glove with Mr Swanson.'

'What in ?' asked Sylvester, returning to earth for a moment. 'Not smuggling. And I bet she wouldn't know an old master if she saw one. I expect they're all quite innocent if the truth were known.'

49

'I'm sure they're not,' said Christiane. 'I've got a "thing" about it. I think it was hearing that ghost. You know, looking back, it sounded fearfully human and real. Not ghostly at all. And, Sylvester . . .'

'What, again?'

'I didn't say anything before, but when we came back all the dust had come back into my room, and there were footprints by the cupboard. I thought it was Ludovic, but just now, when I was talking about the ghost, I suddenly remembered . . . You know how you do see things suddenly, ages after you've actually seen them . . . If you see what I mean . . .'

'I don't,' said Sylvester, 'but go on.'

'Well,' said Christiane, 'those footprints were female. Someone with big feet and highish heels— someone with feet about Miss Penrose's size. It's odd, isn't it? I mean——'

'You're dreaming again,' said Sylvester brusquely. 'And mind that rabbit-hole . . .'

Christiane diverted Scotch from the rabbit-hole, and they rode on in silence for a bit.

'Do you really think I was dreaming?' asked Christiane at last.

'Sure of it,' said Sylvester. 'Dash it all, Chris, it's just silly!'

'Maybe,' said Christiane. 'I suppose it is silly to you—but *I* saw it, Sylvester, and *I* heard the ghost. And anyway, if John didn't think there was something queer about Mr Swanson, why didn't he tell us what he meant about that cave?'

'Maybe he didn't want to,' suggested Sylvester, not very brightly. 'Come on, let's gallop!'

CHAPTER 7

'DID you like the house?' asked Lois, scooping up a handful of silvery sand, and allowing it to run through her fingers, to fall in a little heap on her twin's back.

'Yes,' said Christiane, 'it's lovely. I don't know how you can bear not to live in it.'

'Mmm,' said Lois. She lay back on the sand and stared lazily at Sylvester and Ludovic, who were building an elaborate fort at the far end of the beach.

'Shall we have another swim?' suggested Christiane.

'Too soon after lunch,' said Lois. 'And too hot. Later.'

Christiane began burying John's legs in the sand, for something to do. It was a beautiful cloudless summer day—too good a day, Ludovic had said, to waste it doing nothing, and since the car had arrived the day before, the cousins had all piled in, with bathing things and a picnic lunch, and driven over to Treyarnon Bay for the day.

Christiane decided to go for a walk along the beach by herself. After a few minutes she came to a point where a little path ran up the cliff. She looked at it, wondering if it was worth climbing. It was so hot in the bay, and on the top of the cliff there might be a breeze. And the grass would be cool to lie on, and not nearly so tickly as sand. Christiane slowly began the ascent.

The sun-baked rocks burnt the soles of her feet, and the limpets dug into them. Was it really going to be worth the effort? she wondered. But she was so nearly at the top now it wasn't worth going back. ...

It was just before she reached the top that she heard voices above her.

'They seem to have made a study of it—ghosts here, there and everywhere at their old house, apparently.'

Christiane nearly slipped over the edge. The voice was Miss Penrose's voice, but what was Miss Penrose doing at Treyarnon? Not that she hadn't as much right to be there as Christiane herself. The point was: should she go on, or go back? She wanted to get on to the top of the cliff, but she did not want to meet Miss Penrose. While she was still meditating another voice spoke, and this time the words penetrated.

'It makes it very awkward. You must get them out somehow, before they are sufficiently friendly with the Treleons to hear the story. If they put two and two together and reached the right answer —which wouldn't be hard—they might make things very awkward for us.'

Christiane leaned against the rock for support. She had never heard Mr Swanson's voice, but she was willing to stake all she had that the other speaker was he. And yet—it was too incredible!

'How can I get them out?' said Miss Penrose's voice. 'A more hard-boiled collection of children I've never met. You would have thought a ghost would be enough for most people.'

'But not for them, apparently. Maybe we could bribe them out.'

'How?' demanded Miss Penrose.

'I don't know. ... Wait a minute, though. I have a plan.'

52

' Well ? '

' Sssh ! Someone coming. Shall we go down on the beach, dear Miss Penrose ? '

Miss Penrose murmured an assent. Christiane took one wild look around her, fled down the path, and bounced energetically up again, meeting Miss Penrose and Mr Swanson at the top. All three of them paused and looked at each other. Miss Penrose's mouth dropped open, and she stared as if she couldn't believe what she saw.

' Hullo, Miss Penrose,' said Christiane politely.

' Christiane—my dear ! ' said Miss Penrose, pulling herself together with a visible effort. ' How strange, meeting you here ! I never knew you were thinking of coming.'

' We decided in a hurry,' said Christiane. She pressed herself against the rock while they passed her on the narrow path, and watched them down to the bottom.

' Curiouser and curiouser—as Alice in Wonderland said before me,' she murmured to herself. ' Well, what does A do now ? What would Bert Beanstalk do in a case like this ? '

She went up on to the top of the cliff to think things out a bit, lying on the grass with her hands linked together behind her head, staring up at the wheeling sea-gulls above her against their background of cerulean blue.

I wonder what it would be like to be a sea-gull. To be able to fly miles and miles, and always to be free as air . . . Would it be as nice as being a Christiane Armitage, I wonder ? Christiane !—stop wandering off the point. What are you going to do about Miss Penrose and Mr Swansong ?—no, that's wrong: Swanson. If you tell Ludovic he'll do one

of two things. Either he'll insist on leaving immediately—he never wanted to come really, anyway—
or else he'll say I was asleep; people have been
saying that to me a lot lately.

She sat up with a jerk and hugged her knees,
staring down at the tossing sea against the black
rocks.

Bert Beanstalk would immediately begin detect-
ing. He would detect the fell hand of Phloffelheimer
—I detect the fell hand of Mr Swansong, but that
wasn't difficult. He almost told me. But what is it
all about? Where would Bert Beanstalk begin his
investigations? With Lois and John, I should think.
So I shall—soon. Not today, but tomorrow. Like
Ludovic's motto, " Never do tomorrow what can
be left until the day after, and should have been
done last week ".

'Penny for your thoughts, Chris.'

Christiane looked round in surprise.

'Oh . . . Lois! I thought you were down
below.'

'So I was. I came to find you. Come on—
let's go and have a swim!'

When they got back to the beach they found
Sylvester and Ludovic much as they had been left,
and John wide awake and building a private sand-
castle of his own.

'We're going for a swim,' announced Lois.
'Coming?'

'Of course,' said John. He flung a hand in her
direction and said, ' Pull me up.'

'Lazy!' said Lois, taking hold. She pulled him
on to his knees, and suddenly let go, so that he took
a short-range header into his sand-castle. Lois
giggled.

'Careless!' she said. John scrambled to his feet and chased her, squealing, over to Ludovic and Sylvester. Christiane followed more slowly.

'Hullo,' said Sylvester, looking up from where he was busy digging a wide deep dry moat with a fixed bridge over it. 'Someone sticking pigs?'

'Don't be disgusting,' said Lois. 'We're going to swim. Are you coming?'

'Of course,' said Sylvester. 'Coming, Ludovic?'

'In a minute,' said Ludovic. He was busily engaged in making loop-holes in a wall, which is a delicate business, requiring much care and thought, and so the twins (plural) went off to the pool without him. Lois and John ran on ahead, and Christiane found herself alone with Sylvester, which was always a pleasant thing to be, particularly so in this instance.

'Sylvester,' she said. Sylvester looked at her, waiting. When she said 'Sylvester' in that tone of voice, it usually meant that she had something she was just going to unburden herself about.

'I wasn't dreaming,' said Christiane, making that clear from the start. 'And I overheard a most curious conversation.'

'Tell me,' said Sylvester, so Christiane told him. When she had finished they had reached the pool, where Lois and John were waiting for them, so that Sylvester had no opportunity for comment.

'Come on,' exclaimed Lois. 'Ludovic will be here as soon as you if you walk at that pace!'

'If not before,' said John.

They climbed up on to the rocks and dived into the clear water—three loud splashes and a smaller one. Sylvester had been a diving champion at his school. When they came to the surface again they saw Ludovic sitting on the little dam that blocked the pool's only outlet.

'Hullo,' said Lois. 'That was quick.'

'You mean that you were slow,' said Ludovic.

'Some of us were,' said Lois with meaning.

Christiane cautiously lowered her feet on to the bottom of the pool, and immediately drew them up again with a small squeak, and floated on her back instead.

'Stony,' she commented.

'Well, what did you expect?' asked John. 'An Aubusson carpet?'

'No. Sand.'

'Poor disillusioned little Chris,' said Lois. 'I'm going to do another dive. You might show me, Sylvester. You dive beautifully.'

Lois and Sylvester scrambled up on to the rocks again. John began practising duck-dives, with indifferent success. Christiane and Ludovic swam the length of the pool, side by side, and lay basking on the rocks, watching the divers.

'I'm so glad we came,' said Christiane, dipping a lazy hand into a little pool beside her. 'Look, Ludovic. See how the shells look like jewels under the water . . . and yet they're not nearly so bright when you take them out and dry them in the sun.'

She picked out the loveliest of the shells and made a pool of them beside her: golden and green winkles, orange-striped limpets, and pearly-pink nondescripts like pairs of angel's wings somehow detached from their heavenly owner's shoulders.

'No cowries, though,' she said. 'Cowries are lucky, aren't they?'

'I seem to have heard something to that effect, somewhere,' said Ludovic.

56

'I wish we could live here for ever and ever,' said Christiane. 'I never knew there was a place like Cornwall in the world.'

'*I* wish we could too,' said Ludovic—surprisingly. 'But we can't . . . not unless a miracle happens.'

'And they don't,' said Christiane. 'Not nowadays.' She pushed her shells back into the pool with a splash, and propped herself up on one elbow, the better to see her brother.'

'Would you really like to stay here, Ludovic?'

'If I wouldn't, I wouldn't have said so, would I?'

'No, I suppose not. Oh, how I wish we were rich!'

'We're not poor,' said Ludovic. 'In spite of death-duties and income-tax. We've nothing to complain of at the moment.'

'At the moment!' said Christiane. 'What'll happen when the money from the sale of Stanway runs out?'

'We shall have to augment it,' said Ludovic lightly. 'But there's no need to start worrying yet.'

'N—no,' Christiane concurred. 'But . . . Ludovic, *if* you could leave Sylvester and me and go back into the Navy, could we manage, do you think? Until Sylvester and I were earning?'

'It's not a thing that's likely to happen,' said Ludovic. 'So where's the point in talking about it?'

'But could we?'

Ludovic slid over the edge into the pool.

'I don't know,' he said, and swam away towards the others.

CHAPTER 8

'I'm going to ask them,' said Christiane.

'Ask them what?' asked Sylvester, who had been taken by surprise.

'About Mr Swanson.'

'Who?'

'Mr Swanson.'

'No, not that who. The other who. Them.'

'Lois and John,' said Christiane pityingly. 'You are dense, Sylvester.'

'It's the result of too many sausages,' said Sylvester. 'They blunt the keen edge of my intellect.'

'You mean,' said Christiane, 'the keen edge of your appetite. You never had any intellect.'

'Rubbish.'

'Quite so.'

Sylvester looked at his twin with a sparkling eye.

'Let's go back to the beginning,' he suggested. 'You're going to ask the twins about Mr Swanson. When?'

'Now,' said Christiane. 'If we can find them.'

The twins were in fact coming to find Sylvester and Christiane. They met on the beach.

'How's the kitten?' Lois greeted them.

'Fine,' said Christiane. 'Quite well behaved too. He doesn't like sausage,' she added as an afterthought. Lois, who knew nothing about the sausage diet that prevailed at the cottage, looked blank.

'They don't usually,' she said. 'What have you called it?'

'Him,' said Christiane. 'He hasn't got a name

yet. We can't think of one. We just call it—him—
" Come on " when we want him.'

' Better than Ginger or Diddums or Tibby,' said
Lois. ' Why don't you just call him Come On and
be done with it ? '

' We thought we might all go to St Stephen's
Cove,' said John. ' Can you come? Two of us could
cycle and the other two ride.'

' Good idea,' said Christiane. ' When do we go ? '

' There won't be time to get there before lunch,'
said Lois. ' It's about fifteen miles. We'll have to
go for tea. Don't forget to bring bathing things.'

' If I go home and get the lunch now,' said
Christiane, ' we can have it early, and then we
won't have wasted any time.'

' I'll go and warn Aunt Margaret,' said Lois.
' It's a good thing it's only salad,' she added to
Christiane as they set off ahead of the boys. ' What
have you got ? '

' Fish,' said Christiane. ' I say, Lois, do you
know how to cook chips ? '

' You cook 'em in deep boiling fat until they turn
brown and look done,' said Lois. ' Why ? '

' I wondered,' said Christiane. ' Ludovic said
you just fried the little bits of potato until they were
soft, but I wasn't at all sure that that was the right
way. I'm afraid I'm not much of a cook.'

' I should say not,' said Lois with deep feeling.
' Look here, I tell you what. You go and get the
spuds started, and then I'll come and help you when
I've told Aunt Margaret we'll want lunch early.
I should think you'll all have indigestion as a perma-
nent feature if you go on that way all the time.'

' Golly ! ' said Christiane, awe-stricken. ' Can
you cook ? '

'Aunt Margaret taught me,' said Lois. 'John can too. Have you any parsley?'

'I think there's some in the garden,' said Christiane. 'I'm not sure. But——'

'I'll bring some with me, anyway,' said Lois. 'Just in case there isn't any after all. See you in about ten minutes.' She fled up the street, leaving Christiane standing in a sort of dream on the pavement. However, she recovered very soon and made her way to the cottage, wondering if Lois meant to cook parsley into the chips, or what she meant to do with it. Christiane had met parsley sauce, but she had never connected it with cooking in a cottage.

When Lois arrived at the cottage with her sprig of parsley, she found Christiane in the kitchen, peeling potatoes. The stove was heating up nicely, and although all the windows and the back door were standing open, the heat made Lois recoil.

'Do you mean to say you cook on *that* thing?' she demanded in horror. 'My poor Christiane! and do you call that peeling potatoes?'

'Yes,' said Christiane. Lois put down her piece of parsley and seized the potato and the knife from Christiane's slack grasp.

'Look,' she said, 'you take it off thinly. If you don't you'll have no potato left worth talking about.'

'No,' said Christiane meekly.

'This way,' said Lois, and forthwith proceeded to give Christiane her very first cooking lesson, with the result that Sylvester, when he came in, found not rather burnt dry fish as he had expected from sad experience, but fish and chips just done nicely, with parsley sauce, and fruit salad to follow.

'Goodness!' he exclaimed. 'Been reading the cookery book at last, Christiane?'

'Lois showed me,' said Christiane. 'I must spring it on Ludovic soon. Lois is going to show me how to cook properly. She says we'll get food-poisoning if we go on much longer as we are doing. And, Sylvester—she says there's more than one way to cook a sausage!'

St Stephen's Cove was fourteen and a half miles from Treleon, and a long way away from a road, which meant that the cyclists (Sylvester, with Lois to show him the way) had a long, weary and brambly walk pushing their bicycles after they had cycled the fourteen and a quarter miles that it was possible to cycle. John and Christiane, on the other hand, had a very pleasant time of it with Butter-scotch, and Butterscotch themselves revelled in every minute of it. They arrived first, and began unsaddling Butterscotch, and tethering them to a stunted thorn.

'They'll be all right here,' said John. 'They're lovely, aren't they?' he added, stroking Scotch's neck affectionately.

'Mm,' said Christiane. 'I'm glad we didn't sell them.' She spoke without thinking. John looked at her in surprise.

'Sell them?'

'Yes,' said Christiane. 'We nearly did.'

'Why?' asked John.

'Oh,' said Christiane, 'because . . . just because.'

'All right,' said John. 'I spoke out of turn.'

'I wasn't thinking,' said Christiane. 'Talking to myself. The others are a long time coming, aren't they?'

'They'll be longer yet,' said John. 'Lots longer. Let's wait for them up here.'

They sat on a hillock overlooking the bay for nearly half an hour before they heard a shout behind them, and, turning, were just in time to see Lois put her foot into a rabbit-hole and nearly fall, barking her shins as she did so on the chain of her bicycle. Having seen this, neither John nor Christiane were surprised when Lois's opening remark was:

'Well, did you have a pleasant ride?' Both she and Sylvester looked hot and cross.

'Fine, thanks,' said John. He got up from the hillock and took her bicycle from her.

'We'll stick these under a bush,' he said. 'No-one will ever find them.'

'We've been doing a lot of walking,' said Lois, 'and cycling up hills and so forth. And we're tired. Aren't we, Sylvester?'

'We are,' said Sylvester. But once they had descended to the bay, rested and had a swim, they felt better.

When they had eaten their tea they washed up in a fresh-water spring half-way up the cliff path, and then lay down on the sand to sun-bathe.

Christiane was wondering how best she could open the subject of Mr Swanson. It seemed to be rather a sore point with them, but Christiane wanted to know exactly how she and Sylvester stood with regard to Miss Penrose, and the only way of finding out that she could think of was to ask the twins why they disliked Mr Swanson so.

Of course it might be a mere personal dislike, since he seemed to be not a particularly pleasant man, but on the other hand there might be some very cogent reason for it.

'John and I have been thinking,' said Lois.

'About you and us,' said John. 'You're our cousins, after all.'

'And you might have some ideas on the subject,' said Lois.

'What subject?' asked Christiane and Sylvester, both together.

'The Emeralds,' said Lois—and you could somehow hear that she spoke of them with a capital E. 'The only family heirloom we've got.'

'Ages and ages old,' said John, 'and worth thousands and thousands of pounds.'

'Ah!' said Christiane.

'Why "ah"?' asked Lois.

'Just "ah",' said Christiane. 'You've saved us a lot of trouble,' she added, rolling over on to her front. 'We were going to ask you the same thing—at least not exactly, but I think it'll come to the same thing.'

'We thought you were,' said John.

'We thought it would be less embarrassing if we——' began Lois.

'Lois!' said John. 'Wrong again!'

'I *always* say the wrong thing!' said Lois. 'I never can decide what's right and what isn't, and I always get it mixed.'

'Mixed!' said Sylvester feelingly. 'Perhaps you'd better tell us about these Emeralds.'

'Perhaps we had,' said Lois. 'Less involved.'

'Much less involved,' agreed Sylvester.

CHAPTER 9

THE Treleon Emeralds were, as John had said, extremely valuable, and had been in the family a long time. They were bought by Richard Treleon in 1366 for his eldest daughter, and although they had been re-set time and time again, to keep pace with the changing modes of the centuries, they were, at the time at which the events in this story took place, still the original stones.

It was a tradition in the Treleon family that the Emeralds were given to the eldest daughter of the house at the time of her coming of age, and she kept them until the next eldest daughter came of age. Thus they would belong to Lois when she was eighteen, and she would keep them until any daughter of John's was eighteen, and so on.

The Emeralds were kept in a secret safe at Treleon House. This safe had been installed by an early-eighteenth-century Treleon, and was an ingenious device, concealed behind the mantelpiece in the hall. The mantelpiece had above it a very elaborately carved replica of the family crest, with the family motto, ' Treleon for Treleon ', written below it. The catch that opened the safe was hidden in the carving. It was by no means an original idea, but it worked, which was after all the main thing.

The father of Lois and John, Colonel Treleon, was very poor. He was almost, but not quite, as poor as Sylvester and Christiane's Uncle Bob, but his house was smaller, and he hadn't a large estate or a passion for hunting, and so he had not been forced, like that unlucky baronet, to sell his possessions and throw his house open to public view. Instead he decided to let it.

It was about this time that Mr Swanson first appeared on the horizon. Mr Swanson offered to buy the house at a ridiculously small figure. The Colonel did not wish to sell. Then Mr Swanson offered to lease it for a period of three years, at a rather more reasonable figure. The Colonel agreed. However, before he could close the deal he was taken ill, and his brother William Treleon made all the final arrangements and handed the house over. It was not until the Colonel came home that it was discovered that the Emeralds had somehow got left in the safe.

Colonel Treleon went up to Treleon House to speak with Mr Swanson as soon as he was fit to do so. Mr Swanson was unwilling to let him look in the safe at first, saying that if the safe was hidden so well the Emeralds would be perfectly safe inside it. He said all this with an air of jovial good nature which quite deceived the Colonel, himself a good-natured man. However, jovial or not, the Colonel was determined to get his Emeralds, and in the end Mr Swanson agreed to let him. He stood in the hall while the Colonel opened the safe, apparently engrossed in a magazine which was conveniently lying on the table. He was very surprised when the Colonel found that the Emeralds were not there.

William Treleon was inclined to think that his brother had taken the Emeralds out just before his illness, and subsequently forgotten where he put them, but neither the Colonel himself, nor his children, believed the theory for one minute. The Colonel said nothing, but he made extensive inquiries about Mr Swanson, only to discover that no-one seemed to know the least thing about him.

Colonel Treleon could not, however much he would have liked to, accuse Mr Swanson of stealing the Emeralds. He had no proof for one thing, and for another he could not afford to be sued for libel. He made inquiries at the bank, in case his brother was right, but they told him that he had certainly never put the Treleon Emeralds in a safe-deposit. They were insured of course, but the Colonel did not want to claim the insurance money, because he somehow felt perfectly sure that the Emeralds were not irretrievably lost, and he was determined to get them back. It was unthinkable that the family should lose them after all the centuries that they had remained safe.

John and Lois were quite certain that Mr Swanson was at the bottom of everything, and one day, soon after their father's fruitless inquiry at the bank, they called a council of war behind the wood-shed in Aunt Margaret's garden.

'The first thing to do,' said John, 'is to make sure that we're right. Then we'll have to prove it.'

'How?' asked Lois.

'I don't know,' said John. 'We must think of a way. But the first thing is to make sure.'

'We might be able to do both at once,' suggested Lois. 'Only, perhaps we might need witnesses and things.'

'Rubbish,' said John succinctly. 'If we find the Emeralds we pinch 'em back. He can hardly complain, but he may give himself away somehow, and then . . .'

'We've got to find them first,' said Lois. 'And

so far as I can see there's only one way to do it. We'll have to break into the house.'

'Lois!' exclaimed John in shocked surprise.

'Well, it's our house,' said Lois. 'And our Emeralds too.'

'That's not the point,' said John. 'And it's not our house while old Swansong has it, and it would be most unethical behaviour to break in.'

'It was most unethical of him to steal our Emeralds,' said Lois. 'People who steal ought to expect to have their houses broken into.'

'I don't quite see why,' said John. 'And anyway, if he has stolen the Emeralds the last place they'll be will be the house.'

'*I* don't see why not,' said Lois. 'Where else could he put them?'

'Anywhere,' said John. 'He might even bury them in the ground.'

'You're funking it,' said Lois. 'You're afraid we might be caught. That's what it is!'

'Not at all,' said John. 'I just don't think we ought to break in. Daddy would be furious.'

'Not if we found the Emeralds,' said Lois.

John, however, refused to be convinced, although when asked if he could think of a better plan, he was forced to admit that he could not.

'And, Lois,' he added, 'you're not to go in by yourself. There'd be no end of a scandal if it got known in the village.'

'Why?' asked Lois.

'It's obvious why,' said John. 'Lois, promise me you won't go by yourself?'

'I hadn't thought of it until this minute,' said Lois dreamily. 'No, John, I won't promise. I think it's a very good idea.'

CHAPTER 10

Lois's chance came a few days later, when Mr Swanson went away for the day to Falmouth. Unfortunately John as well as she knew that he was going, and he immediately proposed that they should take a picnic tea and cycle to St Stephen's Cove. Lois agreed, since her father and Aunt Margaret were both present at the time, and it would have looked queer if she had said no; but later on in the morning she accidentally slipped on the steps of the rock-garden and twisted her ankle. After that of course it was unthinkable to cycle fourteen miles, and then climb cliffs.

John was cross with her, but he could hardly blame her for what looked so much like an accident. In fact it looked so much like an accident that John was taken in along with the rest of the household, and that afternoon he unwisely left her in the garden with a book while he went down to the harbour to put in a little rowing practice. The Colonel and Aunt Margaret had arranged to go to tea with the Vicar, and about three o'clock they left the house. The moment the gate had shut behind them, Lois, abandoning all pretence of having hurt herself, skipped out of her deck-chair and ran round to the garage. Five minutes later she was well on the way to Treleon House on her bicycle.

Arriving at her destination Lois pushed her bicycle into the ditch outside the front gate, where the long grass more or less covered it, and dived into the laurel bushes that lined the drive.

Cautiously, avoiding all noise as far as possible, she made her way to the end of the laurels. Ahead of her was a clear space before she reached the house; to her right were the outhouses, and to her left an archway leading on to the terrace.

Having made sure that there was no-one about to overlook her movements, she slipped out of the cover of the laurels and round the corner of the house. There, pressed close against the wall, she took another look round. So far as she could see there was no-one in sight, either on the terrace or the lower lawn. She had no means of telling whether there was anyone in the house; it was a chance she had to take. All the windows overlooking the terrace were closely shut and would, to all outward appearances, have defied the efforts of the most determined of professional burglars, but Lois had been brought up in Treleon House, and knew a few things about it that even the Colonel himself did not know.

Growing close to the house at the far end of the terrace was an oak tree. It had been there a long long time, and was so tall that it was nearly as tall as the house. Lois and John had discovered, fairly early on in their unregenerate youth, that if they climbed up the tree as far as it was safe to do so, and climbed along one of its great branches, they came exactly opposite to, and about a foot away from, a certain small window with a faulty catch. Lois was not sure whether it would be possible for her to get into the house through it now, but she was determined to try.

She ran along the terrace, keeping close to the house to lessen the chances of her being seen from an upper window, and leapt for the lowest branches of the oak. Once fairly concealed among the leaves she felt safer, but fearfully criminal and burglarious. When she had got her breath back she began climbing, until she was opposite the window. Wriggling out along the branch she reached towards the window, and the bough bent under her weight. She shut her eyes, to shut out a vision of the ground rocking to and fro in a most unaccountable manner, and caught hold of the window-frame. The branch steadied itself, and she was able to jiggle the window about until there was a faint click, and it came open under her hand. She lifted it and looked through into a dark little cupboard full of brooms. Then she looked at the smallness of it and the yawning gap between herself and the house, and reflected that she and John had iron nerves when they were small, to be able to use this window even in the dark for getting in and out of the house.

It would only be true to say that Lois, at that moment, would dearly have liked to turn back, were it not for what John would say if she went home with the mission unaccomplished after all the fuss she had made over it. However, having come so far, she told herself, it would be silly to turn back, and she would never have another chance like this again. She laid hold of the window-frame and wriggled forward along the bough. She squeezed her head and shoulders through the window, slid her hands down until she came to the shelf which she knew from long experience was below it, then inch by inch she squeezed through, head first, into the broom cupboard. There was one awful moment when she thought she was stuck, and then she fell with a loud bump on to the floor.

Lois had been terrified all along lest the broom

cupboard should be locked, for nothing would have persuaded her to go back by the way she had come. She intended to leave more decorously by a downstairs window. Luckily, however, the door was open, and she was able to escape from the cupboard into the wider spaces outside.

She stood on the familiar landing a long time, looking down the passage and thinking how queer it was that she, a Treleon of Treleon, should be burgling her own house for her own property. It was a horrible and rather uncanny sensation. She was privately glad that she had had the good fortune to be born into a respectably circumstanced family, and would never have to take up burglary as a profession.

After five minutes' intensive listening she ran along the passage to the head of the stairs, and set her foot cautiously on the first step. Looking over the banisters she could see the deserted hall, with the carving above the mantelpiece and the motto ' Treleon for Treleon '. Treleons had always helped each other, had always defended and upheld each other—and now they were burgling for each other. She ran lightly down the stairs and stood in the hall. Once more every nerve was on the stretch, and her ears were alert for the slightest sound. The house was as still as a church. All she could hear was the solemn ticking of the old grandfather clock in the corner next door to the book-case containing her father's various books on Army History and the *Encyclopaedia Britannica.*

The hall was uncarpeted; her feet made a loud noise on the polished wood, although she was only wearing sandals—flip-flap, flip-flap, all across the hall to the mantelpiece. She stood before the

71

fireplace, looking at the carving and wondering. Then she reached up her hand to the particular piece that opened the secret safe.

Simultaneously the door-bell rang.

Lois let out a gasp of horror. She had no means of knowing if Mr Swanson had left a servant in charge of the house while he was away. That she herself had seen no-one was no proof that the house was empty, because the servants' quarters were on the far side of the house, beyond the outhouses. Quick as thought she dived into the cupboard where, in happier days, the Colonel and his children had been wont to keep their coats and shoes.

For a long time she waited, and there was no sound in the house. Then the door-bell rang again, loudly, imperiously.

Lois waited a little longer, and then slipped out of the cupboard and went cautiously over to the window to see if whoever-it-was had gone. She peered out under the lace curtain, and the next minute had flung up the sash and leaned out. Throwing caution to the winds she called in a mixture of relief and surprise, ' Glyn ! '

The dark young man, who was half-way down the drive, stopped, turned round and looked back. Then he began to retrace his steps. Lois, with beating heart and nervously wobbly hands, waited for him to reach the window.

' Hullo, Lois,' said the young man. ' I rang the bell twice. I thought you must all be out.'

Lois pushed the window open a little wider.

' They are,' she said.

' All but you,' said Glyn.

' Even me,' said Lois. ' Because we don't live here any more.'

Glyn Lloyd had known the Treleons since they were babies and he was a lanky youth of ten, and he had never before had reason to suspect them of being insane. Now however he stood speechless and staring, unable to believe the evidence of his ears.

'I'm burgling,' said Lois. 'Glyn,' she added, 'don't look like that. It's true.'

'I don't believe you,' said Glyn frankly. 'Why should you burgle?'

'We've let the house,' explained Lois. 'And we've lost the Emeralds. I'm just looking for them.'

'John with you?' asked Glyn.

'He wouldn't come,' said Lois. 'He said it was stupid and dangerous.'

'So it was,' said Glyn. 'How did you get in?'

'Through the broom-cupboard window,' said Lois.

'Nonsense,' said Glyn unflatteringly. 'You're too fat.'

'Not in the least,' said Lois.

'You'd better go back through it,' said Glyn, 'if you're *not* too fat. Whatever got into you to go burgling? There'd be the father and mother of a row if it got out that you'd been doing that.'

'But, Glyn—' began Lois.

'Much better get out while the going's good,' said Glyn. 'Come back another time and ask the tenant nicely if you can look for the Emeralds. He'll let you, unless he's an absolute bounder.'

'He is,' said Lois. 'And we have. He says they're not here. Daddy thinks he's stolen them.'

'So?' said Glyn. He sounded interested now, instead of cross.

'Glyn—will you come and help me look?'

'Will I what?'

'Will you come and help me look,' said Lois. 'It'll be so much more comfortable to have company.'

Glyn climbed in through the hall window, and Lois shut it after him.

'I was just going to look in the safe again,' she said. 'Daddy already has, though, and they weren't there.'

They looked in the safe and found it empty. Lois put her hand right in as far as she could reach, but only succeeded in barking her knuckles.

'Where else could he have put them?' asked Glyn.

'There's a secret drawer in Daddy's desk,' said Lois. 'It would be stupid of him to put them there since he must realise that we know of it, but he might have done.'

'I doubt if he was expecting burglars,' murmured Glyn.

'I don't know what else he was expecting,' said Lois.

They went to the Colonel's study together. They both knew the way very well and had no need, as an ordinary burglar would have had, to look into each room to find the right one.

The Colonel's desk was not locked, for John had broken the lock a long time ago while the twins were still almost babies, and it had never been mended. Lois opened a drawer and peered inside.

'We'll have to take all these things out,' she said. 'The secret drawer is right at the back.'

Mr Swanson had filled the drawer with papers and maps, and these Glyn and Lois took out and carefully stacked on the floor beside them. They had just got them all out when a door slammed some-

The door-handle suddenly began turning soundlessly

where in the house. They jumped guiltily and looked at each other, wide-eyed and perturbed.

'Ssh!' said Lois—unnecessarily. 'What was that?' She picked up an armful of papers, ready to push them back into the desk, while Glyn stole over to the door and opened it a crack.

'Female domestic on the distant horizon,' he reported in a whisper. 'Moving in a north-easterly direction towards the stairs.'

'Help!' muttered Lois. 'What shall we do?'

'Lock the door and get on with it,' said Glyn, doing exactly that.

They went all over the desk with a care worthy of any noble cause, without finding so much as one emerald. They were just putting everything back, discussing in low whispers where they should look next, when the door-handle suddenly began turning soundlessly.

'What——' began Lois. Her sentence ended on a quick indrawn breath, as Glyn laid an urgent hand on her arm.

As silently as it had turned the door-handle slipped back again. Someone on the other side of the door said, 'Tch!' and they heard footsteps on the floor of the hall.

'Let's get out of this,' whispered Lois. 'My nerves are in shreds—oh!' She ended on a squeak, as something cold and wet pressed against her leg.

'Quietly,' said Glyn. 'It's only a little pussy-cat. It was asleep in the hearth—I saw it when we came in.'

'O—oh!' said Lois. She tickled the cat behind its ears, and watched Glyn piling papers back in the desk.

'I hope Swansong hadn't a system,' she said. 'If he has he'll notice we've been.'

'Let him,' said Glyn. 'He won't know who we are. I take it you don't want to look anywhere else?'

'I do not,' said Lois. 'I don't believe they're here now, anyway.'

Glyn finished putting the papers back into the desk, and then went over to the window and opened it as quietly as he could—which was rather loudly, for the window was stiff and went up with a bang that brought the atom bomb vividly to mind. Then, while Lois climbed out on to the sunlit terrace, he unlocked the door again and then followed her out. They shut the window as well as they could from the outside, and keeping close to the house and bending below the level of the windows, they made their way to the gap between the house and the laurels. They had to make a dash for it across that, and just as they reached the cover afforded by the bushes, the grey car of Mr Swanson glided up the drive and stopped opposite the front door, and Mr Swanson got out—with Miss Penrose from the village, who was, in the Treleons' estimation, a harmless woman who kept hens.

'Well, strike me down with a feather!' murmured Lois. 'Miss Penrose! What's *she* doing here?'

'Paying a social call,' suggested Glyn, not over-brightly.

'Why?' asked Lois. 'This gets deeper and deeper. But I'm surer than ever that old Swansong has the Emeralds.'

'The point is,' said Glyn, 'where has he put them?'

77

'IT still is the point,' said Lois, now to her cousins. 'We thought and thought, but we just can't think of anywhere he could have put them.'

'But what about our cave?' said Christiane. 'Where did that come into it? When did he say it didn't exist?'

'Oh . . . !' said Lois. 'That was rather queer. John and I were talking to Miss Penrose in the village one day, and she happened to say that "that nice Mr Swanson" was thinking of buying the cottage next to hers, and she said how nice it was that she would have a next-door neighbour again.'

'Lois and I have always wanted to look for that cave,' John took up the tale; 'but since no-one has lived in that cottage for years. we've never been able to ask if we could—well. it stands to reason we couldn't. There was no-one to ask. So we just happened to wonder aloud to Miss Penrose if Mr Swanson might let us look for it.'

'And she said,' said Lois 'that Mr Swanson had made a study of the caves along this coast, because he was writing a book about them, and that cave couldn't possibly exist.'

'Of course,' said John, 'we know it does. One of the most gruesome bits of our family history took place in that cave. It couldn't possibly not exist.'

'Miss Penrose said that Mr Swanson had said that the rock formation or something was all wrong,' went on Lois. 'And no cave could be as deep as that one, and anyway there could be no entrance from the cave to the cottage, because the cave had been there for hundreds of years, and the cottage is quite new.'

' But we know it had an entrance into the cottage that was there before this one,' went on John. ' That's been known for years, because it was used by smugglers and all sorts in the times when smugglers smuggled—— '

' —and all sorts all sorted,' said Lois. ' It was *so* funny, that we asked Mr Swanson. We met him in the village one day, and were terribly terribly polite to him.'

' We told him about the cave,' said John, ' and said that we knew he was a great authority on caves, and did he think there was any chance of its really being there.'

'And he said just what Miss Penrose said he said,' said Lois. ' Why do you want to know, anyway ? '

Christiane and Sylvester between them told the Treleons the full story of the ghost, and the way Miss Penrose had tried to discourage them from living in the cottage, and about the inscription on the wall and the oiled locks, and the footprints in the dust.

' Golly ! ' said Lois. ' I say, you don't think . . . ? '

' What ? ' asked Sylvester. ' It's a very bad habit, not finishing your sentences.'

' That the Emeralds might be there,' said John. ' Oh,' he added, ' but they couldn't be.'

' Yes, they could,' contradicted Lois. ' You heard what Christiane said about the locks and things. They broke in, and put the necklace in the cave.'

' But we were down there, and we didn't see any sign of any necklace,' said Sylvester.

79

'Tell us about this cave,' Christiane commanded. 'I'm rather curious about it.'

'It's just a cave,' said Lois. 'You can only get into it at certain states of the spring tide, except through the cottage, and even at those times it can only be reached by boat. At the ebb of the spring tides is the only time the entrance is uncovered; the rest of the time you can't even see the top of it.'

'When the tide *is* right,' said John, 'you can take a boat and row to the cave, and you row right in and up a sort of passage. That leads to the cave, but it's very dangerous, because if the tide comes up you can be drowned. They say the way to up above is too difficult now for one person to manage.'

'We know!' said Sylvester.

'We've never been there,' said Lois. 'We're not allowed, and we've been made to promise never to go. No-one in the village has ever been either, not even the very oldest fishermen. There's a local superstition about it.'

'Then how do you know about the passage?' asked Christiane.

'Glyn and Mostyn went up it once,' said Lois. 'Mostyn is Glyn's brother, by the way. They didn't even get as far as the cave entrance, because the tide caught up with them, and they were as near drowned as makes no matter. After that they were made to promise too.'

'Who *is* this Glyn person?' asked Sylvester. 'You keep mentioning him.'

'He's a friend of ours,' said Lois. 'His father was a friend of Daddy's, and we've known him all our lives. Him and his brother Mostyn. He knew Mummy, which we didn't, which just shows you.'

'He doesn't live here?' asked Christiane.

'He used to,' said Lois. 'But the Lloyds moved to Wales—they are Welsh, you know.'

'No!' said Christiane sarcastically. 'I don't believe you.'

'Tell us the gruesome bit of history,' Sylvester pleaded. 'You've told us everything about the cave but that.'

'It's a very old bit of history,' said Lois.

'Never mind.' said Sylvester. 'Tell us.'

'Once upon a time,' said Lois, 'long long ago, there was a head of our family who had two children, John and Louise. When they were about fifteen and fourteen he died, and his wicked brother, who had two children of his own, wanted them out of the way, so that he could have Treleon House and his son would be the heir, and his daughter could have the Emeralds. So one day he drugged them and put them in his boat, and took them to the cave and left them there. He had blocked up the passage that led up to the cottage. He meant them to die of slow starvation, but that night there was an awful storm, and when that happens, the water in the cave rises to a height of about seven feet up the walls, so that John and Louise were drowned.'

'Goodness!' exclaimed Christiane. 'I say, was it them who put that carving on the wall, do you think?'

'They did carve on the wall,' said John, 'so that everyone who came afterwards would know how they died. And someone did come, one of their father's old retainers, and he saw the writing on the wall, and he went back and killed the father and the son and the daughter, and so a third brother inherited, and he was our ancestor.'

'How lovely and ghastly!' said Christiane.

'It sounds a good place to put the Emeralds,' said Sylvester slowly. 'But if they *did* put them there, they're in a fix now, because they can't get them out.'

'Unless they feel like rowing in in the dark,' said John; 'which I somehow don't think they will.'

'Why the dark?' asked Lois.

'They'd attract too much attention doing it in daylight,' said John.

'We must get in and look,' said Christiane. 'If the Emeralds are there it shouldn't be hard to find them.'

'It means telling Ludovic about it,' said Sylvester, 'and he'll probably be as sticky as jam about letting us go down.'

'Then we'll have to go some time when he isn't there,' said Lois.

'It's nailed up,' said Christiane.

'Then we must un-nail it,' said John.

'I'm not usually prophetic,' said Sylvester, 'but I see trouble ahead of us. I somehow can't see Ludovic giving in so easily. He's got a " thing " about that cave.'

Sylvester's pessimism proved in the event to be justified. He and Christiane approached Ludovic on the subject next morning at breakfast-time, asking if they might take John and Lois down into the cave and show them. They met, as they had expected, with a blank refusal. Then, in accordance with a prior arrangement, they told the story of the Emeralds. Ludovic looked interested, but unconvinced.

'If they think the Emeralds are in the cave, they'd better tell their father,' he said. 'But they're

82

not going down there without his permission—and neither are you without mine.'

' Oh ! ' said Christiane.

' And,' went on Ludovic, ' there will be no point in your trying to take the nails out, because the door is locked and I have the key.'

Sylvester and Christiane met Lois and John on the beach after breakfast, and told of their unsuccessful mission.

' You'll have to tell your father,' said Christiane.

' We can't do that,' said Lois.

' Why ever not ? ' asked Sylvester. ' It seems the sensible thing to do.'

' For two reasons,' said Lois. ' One is that he probably wouldn't believe us, and the other is that if he did, and the Emeralds weren't there, I think it would be a blow he'd never recover from. You don't understand, Christiane, that the loss of that necklace means so much to him he'd move heaven and earth if he thought it would be a step towards finding it again.'

' You could say what we said to Ludovic,' said Christiane: ' that you want to see the cave, but Ludovic says you can't go down without his permission.'

' I suppose so,' said Lois doubtfully. ' We'll ask at lunch-time.'

Lunch-time came round very slowly that day, and after lunch the Armitages were down on the beach long before the Treleons. The Treleons did not appear until nearly three o'clock, but Christiane and Sylvester knew the instant they saw them that their errand also had met with no success.

' It's hopeless,' said Lois. ' We said what you told us to say first, and Daddy said no with a capital

N. And so we said we thought the Emeralds might be there, and we wanted to look for them, and Daddy said nothing at all, and Aunt Margaret thrust her oar in and called us " silly children ".'

' Oh, blow ! ' said Christiane. ' What does A do now ? '

' Goes in by the back entrance,' suggested Sylvester.

Three voices said in unison:

' What do you mean ? '

' By sea,' said Sylvester calmly.

' But we've promised not to,' Lois reminded him.

' You have,' said Sylvester. ' We haven't.'

There was a short pause.

' But we can't row,' said Christiane.

' We can learn,' said Sylvester. ' We've plenty of time. When's the next spring tide ? '

' Some time at the end of next week,' said Lois. ' But do you think you could learn in that time ? There's a dreadful current, and—— '

' We can try,' said Sylvester.

John laid his hand on the gunwale of the Treleons' rowing-boat, on which the paint was now dry.

' You may as well start right now,' he said. ' Give us a hand here, Sylvester.'

CHAPTER 12

'I'M stiff,' said Christiane, 'and I'm sore, and I've blisters on my hands, and those Treleons won't let us alone!'

'Whatever are they doing to you?' asked Ludovic, surprised.

'They're teaching us to row,' said Christiane, 'and killing us in the process.'

'Good for them!' said Ludovic. 'I was going to teach you myself if I could find the time, but they'll save me the trouble.'

'They don't know how to sail,' said Christiane slyly. 'The boat's got a mast and a sail but they never use it, because they've no-one to show them how.'

'What she means,' said Sylvester, 'is that she thought you might show us.'

'Tell them to choose a calm day and experiment said Ludovic. 'They won't drown if they're careful.'

'Aunt Margaret won't let them,' said Christiane. 'She's a born fusser. It was ages before they were allowed to take the rowing-boat out without a fisherman, although they could row like anything.'

'Very hard for them,' said Ludovic cheerfully. 'All right. I'll teach you—my first free week-end.'

'*Dear* Ludovic,' said Christiane.

'Cupboard love,' said Sylvester. 'Don't listen to her. In proof of how dear you are she's got sausages for supper again.'

'Toad-in-the-hole,' said Christiane, '*a la Lois*. I think it'll be all right.'

'It'd better be,' said Ludovic. 'Any more sausages and I'm leaving home.'

That afternoon Lois and John inexorably dragged their cousins out for some more rowing practice. It was becoming rapidly apparent that the success or failure of the proposed expedition was going to rest with Sylvester, since Christiane was at the moment both weak and wild as far as rowing went. Lois and John, shouting instructions at her, confused her, and the current outclassed her, whereas her twin took both instructions and current in his stride.

'It'll take months to turn you into a passable rower!' groaned Lois on more than one occasion, and even the uncritical John was heard to say that 'Christiane's stroke was rather weak'—which in the circumstances was generous of him.

This particular afternoon Christiane was surpassing herself for inefficiency. It made matters worse when, as they rowed past the fishing-smacks anchored in the harbour, she caught sight of Ludovic leaning on the rail of one of them, looking at her with a stern and critical eye.

'You'll never make an oarsman, Christiane,' he called derisively. 'Go a bit slower, and lift your oars a little higher—That's better.'

Christiane, following his advice, rowed three whole yards with a modicum of success; then once again she failed to lift her oars, and a little wavelet caught one of them and nearly tore it out of her hand. A ribald laugh from the rail of the smack did nothing to restore her self-esteem.

'Oh, Ludovic, shut *up*!' she shouted. 'I know he'll be rude at supper,' she added. 'I just *cannot* row! Sylvester, you take over.'

Sylvester took over, and the rest of the rowing

that afternoon was done by him and Lois and John. Christiane sat in the stern and tried to work out what it was she did wrong, but she did not fathom the mystery until supper-time that evening, when Ludovic solved it for her.

' Too many teachers,' he said when asked what he thought was wrong. 'All criticising and shouting at you, and Sylvester managing so much better and showing you up.'

' Oh,' said Christiane, ' do you think so ? '

' I do,' said Ludovic.

After supper was over (the toad-in-the-hole was an unqualified success, by the way) Ludovic took Christiane down to the harbour, borrowed a boat from one of the fishermen and took her out on the water for a private lesson. Sylvester watched. It was clear that his sister was getting on much better with Ludovic than she did with the Treleons. There was something to be said after all, he reflected, for having ex-naval officers for brothers.

The following day Christiane tried, during her rowing lesson with Lois and John, to put as much of what Ludovic had told her into practice as she could remember, and John went so far as to tell her that she was doing better. Lois wanted to know why.

' Ludovic took her out last night and showed her,' said Sylvester. ' Oh, by the way—we'd forgotten to tell you: he says he'll teach us to sail.'

' Goodness me ! ' said Lois. ' That'll be fine. Jolly nice of him.'

' *Jolly* nice of him,' corroborated John.

' We'd forgotten too,' said Lois: ' we've got to go to London the day after tomorrow, but we'll be back before the tide's right for the cave.'

' We'll go past there this afternoon,' said John,

' and show you where it is. Then if we're not back by some mischance, you'll know where it is.'

' But do be careful,' said Lois.

' I'm not sure we're doing the right thing,' said Christiane, ' but people are so unco-operative. They've left us nothing else to do.'

' There's no danger if you're careful,' said Lois, ' and keep an eye on the tide. Even the Lloyds said that, after they nearly drowned. So long as it's a calm night, and you go at the earliest possible moment, and don't spend a second more than you have to, you'll be quite safe.'

' But we'll be back,' said John. ' We *must* be back, otherwise you won't know the right day. I say, if we're not I don't think you ought to go.'

' Nor do I,' said Christiane. ' I'm pretty sure we oughtn't to go at all, but still . . . '

That afternoon they rowed past the entrance to the cave and could not see it for water, although the tide was nearly at the end of the ebb. In the evening Christiane had another rowing lesson from her brother.

The following day Lois, John, Christiane and Sylvester took the boat and rowed to a small bay down the coast. Christiane and Sylvester did all the rowing.

' That was all right,' said John when they arrived. ' I think you'll do. But practice and practice and practice while we're away.'

That evening Sylvester cut his hand open almost to the bone with the carving-knife, and had to be rushed in the car to the nearest doctor to have it attended to, and the finding of the Emeralds rested entirely with Christiane, the inexpert rower.

CHAPTER 13

CHRISTIANE was exercising Scotch along the beach, which today was entirely deserted. She should have been practising her rowing, according to Sylvester, who took an unholy joy in slave-driving her now that he himself was exonerated, but she had decided that it would be a far better thing to exercise Butterscotch. Butter she had ridden in the morning, and it was now the turn of Scotch.

At the far end of the beach was a cluster of rocky outcrops, and among them was one very big, flat rock. Christiane decided to climb it and sit down for a think. Scotch had had a good deal of exercise anyway. She found a convenient rock to tether the pony to, and climbed up. Once on the top she was completely hidden from anyone walking along the beach from either direction, which exactly suited her. She had a lot to think about.

She was perfectly sure that she and Sylvester and the Treleons were going to get themselves into a situation with which they could not deal, over this cave business. If only they had had the support of Ludovic or the Colonel it would have been different, but as it was they had only themselves to rely on—and the person who would have to take the worst responsibility was herself, and she did not think that she was capable of doing so. To row into a small passage, with a strong current running and only a torch to see by, was a feat beyond her power to execute—of that she was more than certain. But if she did not do it there was no-one who could.

It was a boiling hot day, with a thundery sort of heat that seemed to advertise the fact that the fine weather was about to come to a damp and noisy end. But for the moment the sunlight was so pleasant on her face, that Christiane's problems gradually slid away from her, and she fell into a state that was half sleeping and half waking.

She was disturbed by someone beside the rock breaking into song in a foreign language that sounded like German. Wakened to life she rolled cautiously over on to her front, and peered over the edge of the rock to see what she could see.

The singer was a young man in a check shirt and grey slacks, who was leaning against the rock and drawing in the sand with a long thorn stick.

After a few minutes the singing stopped, and Christiane looked over the edge of the rock again. The singer was now writing his name in the sand, and Christiane read it over his shoulder.

GLYN she read, and suddenly a simply stupendous idea came into her head, so stupendous that before she could stop herself she said, ' Oh ! '

Glyn looked up in surprise, and stared at her for a long time.

' Hullo,' said Christiane. He smiled at her and the fixed stare faded.

' Hullo, Rusty,' he said. Christiane sat up.

' I say,' she said, ' you don't happen to be Glyn Lloyd, do you ? '

' What of it ? ' he asked.

' I'm the Treleons' cousin,' explained Christiane. ' I've heard you mentioned from time to time.'

' Yes,' he said. Christiane looked at him frowningly.

'You're not a fearfully good conversationalist,' she observed.

'Give me a chance,' he protested. Christiane began climbing down the rock.

'Jump,' he suggested. 'I'll catch you.'

Christiane jumped, and true to his word Glyn caught her. He recoiled a little under her weight.

'No fairy, are you?' he said feelingly.

'No fairy at all,' said Christiane. 'But it was your suggestion that I jumped.'

'Never again,' he said. Christiane pulled a face at him.

'Considering that you've only just met me, you're not terribly polite,' she said.

'I keep thinking you're Lois,' he apologised. 'You sound like her. And I've known Lois since she was the size of an acorn.'

'Do I sound like her?' asked Christiane, astonished.

'Very like her,' said Glyn. There was a short silence, while Christiane tried to work out the best way of leading up to what she had to say. In the end she spilt everything out in one wild burst.

'If you are you, you must know about the Emeralds disappearing, and we're in the most awful fix,' she said, all in one breath.

'Most certainly I'm me,' he replied. 'And I do know about the Emeralds, and I'll do anything to help you find them except more burgling. Once was enough as far as that went.'

'Well,' said Christiane, 'it's a long story—and rather private.'

'We can walk up and down the beach while you tell me,' said Glyn. 'Then the villainous Mr—what was his name?—won't hear us.'

'Or his accomplice, the feeble Miss Penrose,' said Christiane. 'I overheard them, but I'd rather they didn't return the compliment.'

'What *is* his name?'

'Swanson,' said Christiane.

They walked slowly up and down the long stretch of beach, and as they walked Christiane told Glyn the whole story from the beginning, when they had first come to the cottage, to the end, which was her twin's lamentable accident with the carving-knife. Except to ask a few necessary questions about who was who, her audience was quiet and attentive.

'And what do you want me to do?' he asked at the end.

'Come into that beastly cave with me,' said Christiane. 'If I go alone I'll get drowned for sure, and the others can't come because they promised not to. With you, now you're grown up, we could always get up the steps if it came to the worst.'

'I don't mind coming,' said Glyn. 'But do you think it's quite the right thing to do? I should have thought your brother and the Colonel would rather you went in in the usual way from the cottage.'

'But I told you,' said Christiane; 'they won't let us.'

'I bet they would if they knew what you intended to do instead.'

'If they did know,' said Christiane, 'they'd make us promise not to, as well as the others, and then we'd be caught all ways. I know Ludovic.'

'And I suppose if you tried to blackmail the Colonel, Aunt Margaret would step in?'

'Undoubtedly,' said Christiane. 'I think she

thinks we're playing some complicated game, and that we're about ten.'

' She probably does,' said Glyn. ' She still treats me as if I was about fourteen or so.'

' I'm fourteen,' said Christiane, with a faintly antagonistic note in her voice.

' I beg your pardon, Rusty,' he said. ' For fourteen read twelve throughout. That better ? '

' Much better,' said Christiane. ' But why do you keep calling me Rusty ? '

' I've got to call you something,' Glyn apologised. ' You see, you have the advantage of me. You know my name, but I haven't an idea what yours is.'

' Christiane Armitage,' said Christiane. ' Not Christine,' she added, ' although most people call me that for ages.'

' Christine—iane, sorry,' said Glyn. ' What a mouthful ! Shall we stick to Rusty ? I shall never remember that " iane " business.'

' Perhaps we'd better, then,' said Christiane. 'Aunt Margaret always calls me Christine, and then corrects herself and calls me Christina.'

' I can sympathise with her,' said Glyn. ' But she never does remember names quite correctly. She calls me Glen, as if I were a valley. And she calls Mostyn Martin. Mostyn is my elder brother.'

' Yes, Lois told me,' said Christiane.

' Is there anything Lois didn't tell you ? '

' Not much, I shouldn't think.'

' Oh well, she always was a chatterbox,' said Glyn. ' She and John—they talked the hind leg off a donkey ! '

' They still do,' said Christiane. ' I wish we knew when they were coming home,' she added, reverting without warning to the original conversation. 'Or even where they are. But they forgot to leave their address.'

'Careless of them!' said Glyn. 'You'll have to talk to them about it when they come back. In the meantime we'd better be thinking out the best way to get into the cave.'

'I say—' said Christiane suddenly, 'poor Scotch. I'd forgotten all about him!'

'Scotch?'

'My pony,' explained Christiane. 'I left him by the rock.'

They walked back to rejoin the deserted Scotch, slowly, talking over ways and means of getting into the cave.

'Would it be very dangerous going by sea?' asked Christiane.

'Not particularly,' said Glyn. 'Not if you chose the tide right, and the sea was calm.'

'That's what Lois said,' said Christiane. 'She and Sylvester don't seem to think there's any danger at all, but I do—and so does John.'

'It'll be all right so long as we're careful,' said Glyn. Christiane noticed the 'we' with a deep thankfulness.

'If you're coming I'm not so worried,' she said. 'It was only when you weren't I was.'

'Quite,' said Glyn.

'What I mean,' began Christiane, and then decided that it might be better not to try to explain. 'Never mind,' she finished hurriedly. 'But I'm glad you're coming.'

CHAPTER 14

It was August Bank Holiday and the train from London to Exeter was very crowded, so that although the Colonel and Aunt Margaret were able to find seats, Lois and John had to travel sitting on their cases in the corridor. They did not particularly mind, for both of them hated London with a great hatred, and would have happily gone home sitting on the buffer if there had been no other way.

' I wonder how Christiane and Sylvester are getting on with their rowing,' Lois said.

' Lucky beasts ! ' said John.

' Why ? '

' Rowing on the sea in peace and quiet, while we're all muddled up with a pack of hooligans— hoy ! That was my foot ! '

' Was it ? ' asked the boy who had stepped on him, and went on pushing his way up the corridor.

' Yes,' said John, ' it was. Of course,' he added, ' it's bad manners to say you're sorry when you tread on a person's foot.'

The boy was out of hearing of this pearl of sarcasm, and so it was entirely wasted.

' No-one has any manners nowadays,' said Lois. ' Listen to Aunt Margaret sometimes.'

' I already listen to her quite often enough,' said John.

' I hope they're getting on all right,' said Lois, reverting unexpectedly to the original conversation. ' But I expect Christiane has drowned them both.'

' See the papers this morning ? ' asked John suddenly.

' No,' said Lois.

' It said,' said John, ' that the north coast of Cornwall was being swept by the most dreadful freak storms, and it was raining fit to bust all the time. Which sounds to me rather unhopeful.'

' Oh goodness ! ' said Lois. ' It sounds awful. Christiane needs such a lot of practice, even with Ludovic to coach her.'

' They'll have got some in before the weather broke,' said John. ' What I'm worried about is, what if the weather isn't better by the spring tides ? '

' Wait,' said Lois. ' They'll come round again.'

' Next spring's is the lowest tide of the year,' said John. 'A wonderful opportunity—if we can take it.'

' The old smugglers used to manage all right all the year round,' said Lois.

' They had some practice,' said John. 'And even they didn't go into the cave in a storm, or if the sea was the least bit rough—it says so in that book Daddy's got at home.'

At Exeter, where they changed trains, it was raining, a steady grey downpour, and they noticed more and more wind as they drew near Plymouth. The hearts of the twins sank correspondingly but when they arrived at Treleon in the early evening, they found that it was not raining at that particular moment; and although there was a great deal of wind there was also a pale watery sun in a cloudy sky. A great black cloud was on the horizon, promising more rain to come within the next hour or two.

' Horrid ! ' said Lois. ' You wouldn't think it was the beginning of August, would you ? '

'You certainly wouldn't,' agreed the Colonel. 'Disgusting weather!'

As soon as they had shed their coats and laid the table for supper, Lois and John dashed out to visit the Armitages, to tell them that they had returned. However, they met them in the road.

Christiane and Sylvester were sitting on their garden fence, while Glyn carefully backed Ludovic's red car, now decorated with conspicuous L-plates, down the road. Ludovic sat beside him with an apprehensive frown on his face.

'Hullo,' called Christiane. 'I didn't know you were back! Ludovic is teaching Glyn to drive.'

'We came back this evening,' said John.

'*Who* to drive?' asked Lois.

'Glyn,' said Christiane. 'Your burgling friend.'

The car same to a sudden and to most people unexpected stop.

'We're going to the cinema tonight,' said Sylvester. 'There's a good film on, for a wonder.'

'Glyn's going to drive us,' said Christiane. 'We might see you tomorrow.'

'Might?'

'If we're still alive,' explained Christiane.

Glyn and Ludovic climbed out of the car and came over to them.

'Glyn!' said Lois. 'We didn't know you were coming.'

'If you remember,' said Glyn gently, 'I wrote and told you. Last May.'

'And we haven't heard a word from you since then,' said Lois. 'No wonder we forgot! Have your mother and father and Mostyn come too?'

'Not Mostyn,' said Glyn, 'but everyone else. Mostyn couldn't get away.'

'What, over August Bank Holiday?' said John.
'I thought everyone had a holiday then.'

'Not hotel owners,' said Glyn. 'It's the busiest time of the year for them.'

'Well,' said Lois, 'he *would* keep a hotel. How long are you here for?'

'A fortnight,' said Glyn. 'We've had half of it already.'

'And we were away!' said Lois. 'What a sell!'

'Sylvester,' said John suddenly.

'What?' asked Sylvester, although he knew perfectly well what was coming.

'What have you done to your hand?'

Sylvester glanced down at the hand in question, which was reposing interestingly in a sling.

'There was a slight accident,' he said, 'with the carving-knife.'

'Oh . . . !' said Lois.

'It rather dished the rowing practice,' said Christiane, 'but I'm getting on fine. Glyn's been helping me.' She intended this remark to contain a double meaning, but she was not sure if it had. Lois, to be sure, looked much struck with the idea, but John was looking merely miserable. Christiane wished that Ludovic had not been there, so that she could put John out of his misery.

'We're going to be late for supper,' said John, glancing at his watch. 'We'll see you tomorrow—if you're still alive!'

'We shall be,' said Ludovic. 'He's quite good.'

'He's had four lessons,' said Christiane. 'All from Ludovic. Sylvester and I are frightened.'

'You've no need to be,' said Glyn with dignity. 'I had one lesson from Mostyn and one from a driving-school at Chirk before this.'

'That's six all together,' said Lois, doing some quick mental arithmetic. 'Well, it sounds safe—but I wonder if it is?'

'Perfectly safe,' said Ludovic. 'He'll be taking his driving-test soon—possibly.'

'I don't quite like the "possibly",' said Lois. 'Oh well, *adieu* or *au revoir*, whichever suits the case by tonight.' She and John set off down the road, running as fast as they could. The others went into the Armitages' cottage for a quick supper before leaving for the pictures.

It was such a miserable evening that the Armitages and Glyn, when they arrived at the cinema, found a queue yards long. They had meant to arrive in good time, but owing to unforeseen difficulties in parking the car they arrived very much later than that.

'We'll never get in at this rate,' said Ludovic gloomily. 'I don't know why we came. It's pouring with rain, and it would be much nicer at home.'

'Grumbler!' said Christiane. 'Whose suggestion was it, anyway?'

'*I* thought it was yours,' said Ludovic.

'Oh!' said Christiane. 'Perhaps it was.'

The commissionaire came along the queue, calling out:

'Two seats in the middle circle. Anyone want two seats in the middle circle?' He paused when he reached Glyn. 'Two seats in the middle circle, sir,' he said, 'if you and the young lady would like them.' He did not seem to connect Glyn and Christiane with Christiane's brothers.

'Better go,' said Ludovic. 'Sylvester and I will

get in where we can. We may be able to join up inside.'

' Right,' said Glyn. ' Come on, Rusty.'

He and Christiane left the queue and dived into the cinema out of the rain. Glyn had to pay for Christiane's seat, since Ludovic, who had intended to pay, had forgotten to give her any money.

'They probably all think I'm taking my girl friend out on a spree,' said Glyn as they went up the stairs.

' Let them,' said Christiane. ' I've never been taken out by anyone but Sylvester or Ludovic—oh, and Billy, once.'

' Who on earth was Billy ? ' asked Glyn.

'A boy I knew at school,' said Christiane. ' He took me out to tea at a sort of roadhouse, and we had buns, and tea in thick cups, and after that he took me up on the Downs and proposed to me. I was seven at the time, and he was about ten. But he never took me out again, although we were engaged—I suppose we still are, because I never gave him his ring back.'

' He gave you a ring, then ? '

' Oh yes,' said Christiane. ' Tin, and the stone was the very best glass—bright blue and sort of chippy. I've still got it somewhere.'

' Interesting relic,' said Glyn.

By this time they had reached the door that led into the auditorium, and an usherette was demanding their tickets in a hushed and urgent whisper.

They had come in half-way through the secondary film, which was a rather gloomy affair, of which neither of them could make head or tail. There were three men, and a girl who appeared to be in love with two of the men at once; and before the end the third man, who was also in love with the girl, shot himself and she ran away with one of the other men, and the last one went into a monastery.

'Nasty piece of work that girl,' said Glyn when the film was over.

'I liked the one who went into the monastery best,' said Christiane. 'But it was a bit weak-kneed of him.'

'Utter rubbish, the whole thing,' said Glyn sweepingly

'Some people like that sort of thing,' said Christiane.

'I don't. Do you?'

'No, said Christiane. 'I wonder if Ludovic and Sylvester have got in yet? I can't see them anywhere.'

'Neither can I,' said Glyn, 'but they may be downstairs.'

At that moment the lights went down and advertisements began to flash on the screen.

'Oh bother!' said Christiane. 'Now we shan't be able to see.'

'See what?' asked Glyn. 'The film or the others?'

'The others,' said Christiane.

They stopped talking to watch an advertisement for Pinkum's Patent Penwipers, which was not particularly thrilling. Christiane's mind was beginning to wander; subconsciously she was listening to fragments of conversation around her.

'And, my dear,' said a voice to her left, 'if I told Mabel once I told her a thousand times. *Gladys is difficult to live with.*'

'I said to him,' said someone else, "If you do

anything of the kind you're no son of mine." And he went straight off and married her ! '

' Dreadful ! ' said another voice.

' Hot lemon and honey is the thing,' said someone farther down the row, but what hot lemon and honey was the thing for, Christiane never discovered, for at the same time someone behind her said:

'And that girl and her brother—Christiane, and something queer—we can get rid of them the same way, and then we can get it easily. But we must do it soon.'

' It'll make a very dull day for you,' said someone else, ' and probably they won't accept. And there's another brother.'

' He's out all day, anyway,' said the first voice. ' Hush now. We don't want to say anything more.'

'A cinema is the safest place on earth for discussing secrets,' said the second voice. ' Nobody ever listens. We must get all this quite clear, because we can't discuss it again. If the other brother *isn't* out—he sometimes isn't, I believe—what then ? '

' He can be disposed of—somehow,' said the first voice. ' I leave that to you.'

The Gladys and Mabel people began talking again then, and the rest of the conversation was lost; but Christiane had heard quite enough. She glanced at Glyn to see if he had heard too, but he appeared to be engrossed in an advertisement for Simmond's Super Orange Squash. She could not say anything to him then and there, for obvious reasons.

It was lucky, she reflected, that she was wearing a scarf over her rusty-coloured hair, because at least one of the men behind her would be able to recognise her immediately by that alone. She must be careful not to let them see her face at all. They did not know Glyn so far as she was aware, and probably they would think, like the commissionaire and the usherette, that he was just a young man of no consequence taking out his girl.

The film was a good one, but Christiane did not enjoy it as much as she might have done. She was frightened all the time of what might happen if either of the men behind her caught a glimpse of her face and recognised her. One of them she did not know at all, but he might have seen her or had her pointed out to him; and if she were recognised the fat would be in the fire with a vengeance. Not that they could do anything to her in a crowded cinema, and she did have Glyn to defend her; but, and it was a big ' but ', if she were seen, and they thought she had overheard them, they would change their plans. While at the moment she had only a faint idea of what to do, her luck in over-hearing the plans of Mr Swanson and his accom-plices had been phenomenal on two occasions, and she couldn't expect it to happen three times.

When the film was over she held Glyn up by pretending to have lost her handkerchief, until the row behind them was almost deserted; then she raised a flushed and rather frightened face to his, and said in a low voice:

' That was Mr Swanson behind us, and he was making plans with someone else to get us out of the way, and I think he was going into the cottage for the cave, which proves that the Emeralds are somewhere there, and oh, Glyn, whatever can we do ? '

CHAPTER 15

THERE was no chance for Christiane to say more in the cinema; they were being swept in a sea of people towards the exit, and also they were trying to locate Ludovic and Sylvester, who were still nowhere in sight, and such conditions are not ideal for plotters and planners.

Outside the doors of the cinema it was pouring with rain. Rain ran gurgling in the gutters, dripped from the roofs and danced on the pavements. Christiane and Glyn stood dripping wet, and growing wetter every minute, waiting for Ludovic and Sylvester to appear.

' What *are* they doing ? ' said Christiane. 'And wherever did they get to ? '

' I wish they'd buck up,' said Glyn. 'We'll catch our deaths of cold standing here.'

' We should have waited inside,' said Christiane, ' except that we should probably have missed them —oh ! ' She caught Glyn's arm and dragged him out of the light streaming from the open doors into the shadows beyond. Mr Swanson and another man passed within a foot of them, laughing and talking about the film they had just seen. The stranger looked at them as he passed, without interest, a cool impersonal stare. Christiane looked down at her feet.

' That's Mr Swanson,' she said in a low voice. ' Don't let him see you.'

' It wouldn't matter much if he did,' Glyn pointed out; ' he doesn't know me.'

' I thought he'd see me for sure in the cinema,'

said Christiane. ' Glyn—before Ludovic appears—
what can we do if he tries to get into the cottage ? '

' He can't, while you're there,' said Glyn.

' He said he'd " get rid of us the same way ",'
said Christiane, ' and he was going to leave it to
the other man to put Ludovic out of the way if he
was still there—and I don't think he meant to do it
gently.'

' We'll just have to wait and see what happens,'
said Glyn. ' If we take care that Mr Swanson never
sees us together, I can keep an eye on the cottage if
and when he tries to get you out of the way. But
we can't very well decide what to do until we know
what *he's* going to do. He can't kidnap you, so he'll
have to give some warning.'

' I wouldn't put it past him to kidnap us,' said
Christiane.

' What, all four of you ? ' asked Glyn. ' I take
off my hat to him if he thinks he can succeed in
doing that.'

' I suppose it might be a bit difficult,' said
Christiane.

' It might ! ' agreed Glyn. ' Hullo, here are the
others.'

' Wherever did you two get to ? ' asked Christiane
moving forward into the light again. ' We looked
all over the place.'

' Standing-room only in the stalls,' said Ludovic.
' How did you get on ? '

' We had jolly good seats,' said Christiane. ' Did
you enjoy the film ? '

' It was jolly good,' said Sylvester. ' Need we
stand here in the rain, though ? Ludovic and I have
been standing all the evening, and we're bored
with it.'

They walked in the rain to where they had parked the car. There was not a star in the sky, and no moon. The rain teemed down in sheets, and by the time they reached the car they were all soaking wet.

' Flu for four ! ' said Ludovic.

They reached the cottage with great thankfulness at eleven o'clock, having dropped Glyn at the *Fishing Smack* as they passed. Christiane made some cocoa on the kitchen stove, while Ludovic put the car away. It was kept at the end of the road, in the gate to the field, under a tarpaulin cover, and by the time Ludovic had finished struggling with wet tarpaulin that was being blown about in the wind, so that it would not stay where it was put, he was not in a very good temper. He walked into the kitchen looking stormy-eyed and cross, and glared at his cocoa as if it was arsenic. Christiane and Sylvester sat side by side on the kitchen table, Christiane holding the kitten, who was purring like an aeroplane.

' Poor little Come On ! ' she crooned to it. ' Have we deserted you then, and left you lonely all the evening ? '

' If you're not careful,' said Sylvester, ' you'll grow up into one of those awful women who have Pekineses called Diddumsiddims, with pink bows round their necks and that snuffle and snort and yap, and are fed on chocolate biscuits and caviar.'

' The women or the Pekineses ? ' asked Christiane.

' The Pekineses,' said Sylvester. ' What are you glooming about, Ludovic ? You look like a wet haddock.'

' It's the weather,' said Christiane. ' It's getting on his nerves, isn't it, Ludovic ? '

'Partly,' said Ludovic; he put his cup down on the table with a bang. 'I'm sorry, twins,' he said; 'we're leaving here at the end of the summer.'

There was a stricken silence from the table.

'But—why?' asked Christiane at last. 'Don't you like it here, Ludovic?'

'I've told you before,' said Ludovic, 'yes. But we're still leaving.'

'Why?' demanded Sylvester.

'Because we've got to live somehow,' said Ludovic. 'You two have got to go to school somewhere, and I'll have to earn the money to send you there. And as I've no training of any kind I'll have to get some, which means living in a town, preferably London.'

'But, Ludovic,' wailed Christiane, 'I thought you'd liked being a fisherman.'

'I have,' said Ludovic, 'but baronets aren't fishermen, and they never can be, I've discovered.'

'Why not?' asked Sylvester.

'Because the other men in the fleet don't like it,' said Ludovic. 'They're inverted snobs.'

'East is east and west is west sort of thing,' said Christiane. 'Surely there's something else you could do here, Ludovic? Why, if we lived in London we couldn't have Butterscotch or Come On, or swim every day, or go sailing with Lois and John or—or anything.'

'What else could I do?' asked Ludovic. 'Be a ploughman, or hand out beer at the inn?'

'What would you be in London?' asked Sylvester. 'And where would we live?'

'We could get a flat somewhere,' said Ludovic.

'Oh!' said Christiane. She stared miserably down at her cup. 'What would you do?'

'Get some sort of training,' said Ludovic;
'clerical work or something'

'And work in a bank all day?' said Christiane.

'Probably—in the end. I always was good at
figures.' Ludovic gave a dreary little laugh.

'And when we grow up,' said Christiane,
'Sylvester and I will be steeped in business too,
helping make the rush at the rush hour, and
spending our days in the office, coming home every
evening to a flat which will probably look out over
a garbage-dump. Ludovic—we can't!'

'Don't exaggerate,' said Ludovic. 'It wouldn't
be anything like that.'

Christiane hugged the kitten so hard it mewed
in protest.

'But, Ludovic, it *would*!'

'Fancy living in a town!' said Sylvester.
'Particularly London—dirt and noise, and hordes
of people—after living here.'

'Where there are hardly any people,' said
Christiane, taking up the tale of woe, 'and all our
friends like John and Lois, and the Colonel, and
the Lloyds—and even Aunt Margaret!—and the
landlord's wife and the butcher. And there's the
country all round us, and the sea and the ships.
Ludovic, you'd hate it as much as we would.'

'I do wish you two would stop *complaining*,' said
Ludovic, rising to his feet. 'No, Christiane, I
wouldn't like it, and I won't like it and I'll loathe it,
but we've got to do it or we'll all be in the poor-
house.' He went out of the kitchen, slamming the
door behind him. Christiane and Sylvester sat still
on the edge of the table. Christiane spoke first.

'Sylvester—we mustn't let him do it. Just think
how awful it would be! It's unthinkable!'

'But we can't stop him,' said Sylvester. 'And he's right, you know.'

'He is not!' said Christiane. 'He's wrong, and he's wrong, and he's wrong! Sylvester, we'll all hate living in London.'

'What do you suggest doing about it, then?' asked Sylvester.

'I don't know,' said Christiane, 'but we must do something.'

'There's not even anyone we can ask. We've no relations.'

'Except the Treleons, and they've troubles of their own.'

'We must work it somehow,' said Sylvester. 'We can't ask Cousin Lizzie—she wouldn't understand.'

'We'll have to find some way for us to settle in the country somewhere—preferably here,' said Christiane. 'Then Ludovic can go back into the Navy, and we can all live happily ever after.'

'Sounds perfect,' said Sylvester. 'But how can we do it?'

'I don't know,' said Christiane. 'Sylvester, please go away and leave me with the washing-up, because I'm sure I'm going to howl, and I'd rather do it alone.'

CHAPTER 16

BERT BEANSTALK was in another unenviable situation. This time he was drifting out to sea in a small boat in a storm, with no oars, and the shore was too far away for swimming. Since Christiane had met Lois and John her hero's adventures had taken on a nautical flavour; unfortunately, however, this had given so much more scope to that master of crime, Phloffelheimer, that poor Bert was in imminent danger of coming to a watery and premature end.

Phloffelheimer had surpassed himself this time [she wrote]. *He stood on the shore shaking with laughter, and watching the tiny speck that was his enemy's boat drifting farther and farther out to sea. Faintly over the water he heard the shrill frightened bark of Beanstalk's little German sausage-dog—a fellow countryman. It says much for his villainy that he felt no pang of compunction or regret.*

Christiane put down her exercise-book and lay on her back. It was a heavenly day, cloudless and warm, with hardly a breath of wind. The little cove where they were spending the day was small and sheltered, and perfect for bathing. The sand was silver, the sea and the sky were green and blue respectively—in fact, thought Christiane, everything was exactly the right colour, and there were only two things to spoil a wonderful day. One was the thought that the summer was gradually coming to an end. and the other was that the next day was the lowest tide of the year.

She gave herself a shake and began to write again:

'Ha ha !' ecxlaimed Phloffelheimer, ' now he is really caught ! Nothing can save him now ! However he had reckoned without the courage and resource of his foe, who tied the poor little dog to the painter of the boat, put him overboard and urged him to swim to land. Sausage-dogs are shaped like buoyancy tanks, for which reason his brilliant plan succeeded and he was saved.

'Although,' said Christiane aloud, ' if it was too far for Bert to swim, it must have been much worse for the poor little dog.'

' Is he going to get wherever it is in time ? ' asked Sylvester. ' Or will the villainous Phloffelheimer succeed in stealing the Crown Jewels, and become the richest man in Europe ? '

' Of course he'll be in time,' said Christiane; ' he always is. It wouldn't be right if he wasn't.'

' I'm sure it must be tea-time,' said John. ' We'll have to have it fairly early, anyway, if we're going shrimping at Polgith Bay.'

' Let's have another bathe before tea,' suggested Lois. ' By the time we've done that it'll be about the right hour.'

' Good,' said Christiane. ' I'm hot. I'll come in with you.'

' Me too,' said John. ' You *would* go and hurt your hand. Sylvester ! You could have given us a diving lesson.'

The three of them. John, Lois and Christiane, ran down to the sea and plunged in with three splashes and three shouts. Sylvester, having

nothing better to do than watch them—which was
tantalising—picked up his twin's exercise-book and
read through what she had written. Then he picked
up her pencil . . . .

It was nearly half an hour before hunger drove
the others out of the water. and when they eventually did come out they found that Sylvester had
collected all the wood for the fire, had lit it and
was watching the kettle boil.

'Good!' exclaimed Lois. 'Just what I want!
John, you're sitting on my towel!'

'Oh. am I?' said John. He stood up passed
Lois her towel and sat down again.

'My exercise-book!' shrieked Christiane. 'Oh,
you clumsy oaf!'

She rescued *The Adventures of Bert Beanstalk* from
beneath John, shook the sand out of its pages and
spread the book on her knees. Then she suddenly
became as still as a statue. Her eyes were fixed on
her book. Sylvester was carefully occupied in
brushing sand off his sandwich.

'It's a good name for them,' said Lois watching
him.

'What is?' asked John.

'*Sand*-wiches,' said Lois.

'Sylvester,' said Christiane, 'I accuse you of
infringement of copyright.'

'Me?' said Sylvester. 'What have I done?'

'Let me see,' said Lois, holding out her hand.
'Has he been writing your story for you?'

Christiane passed over the exercise-book. open
at the right page. There was a bit at the top of the
page in Christiane's tidy writing, and then a long
bit written in Sylvester's scrawl—all the worse
because he was left-handed, and his left hand was

the one that had suffered from the carving-knife episode.

This is what Lois read:

While Bert Beanstalk was giving his magnificent brain some unaccustomed exercise, Phloffelheimer had been busy. He had run to the nearest road and held up a postman at the point of a gun, then seizing the postman's bicycle and very untidily leaving the poor man in the middle of the road, all tied up, he proceeded to pedal at top speed to the Royal Palace. Once there he left his bicycle (or rather the postman's bicycle) in an empty sentry-box, and crept towards the moat, into which he dived, like John, with a splash. He had not noticed that the drawbridge was down and unguarded.

Once on the far side he crept along the walls until he came to the back door, which stood open. He slipped inside and found himself in the kitchen. Helping himself on the way to a large raw turbot which he found on the table, he made his way, chewing ravenously, to the chamber where the Crown Jewels were kept. The tail of the turbot was just sliding pleasantly down his gullet as he reached it. Fortified with this stolen meal he slipped inside the door, shot the sentry on duty, broke the glass of the case where the Jewels were kept, and made his escape the way he had come. However, his luck was out! As he came into the kitchen he heard a bark and a snuffle, and there to his horror was the German sausage-dog of Bert Beanstalk, snarling and growling at him. Since Phloffelheimer had taken (I forgot to mention it before) the postman's uniform for disguise, the dog was misled and thought he was the postman. Phloffelheimer let out a shout of rage and made to draw his gun, when he suddenly realised that he had left it in the glass case where the Jewels had

been. Simultaneously with the realisation, Bert Bean-
stalk appeared in the doorway, dripping wet; he also
had not noticed that the drawbridge was down.

'It's not as good as Christiane's,' said Lois.
'You've made it too improbable. Why the turbot?'

'I don't know,' said Sylvester. 'Maybe he liked
raw turbot. Anyway, the dog had it in for him
because he had turned traitor and marooned his
own countryman in a boat with a paltry English-
man.'

'That doesn't explain the turbot,' said John.
'What's the whole thing all about, anyway?'

Lois passed him the book.

'He never took the Crown Jewels,' she said.
'He just broke the glass and went. I call it very
silly of him, after all that trouble.'

'Me too,' said Christiane. 'Pass me another
sandwich, Lois.'

As soon as tea was over they packed up, stamped
out the fire, buried all the rubbish and re-embarked
in the boat. Lois and Christiane were doing the
rowing this time, with John and Sylvester to cox
and make rude remarks.

'You'd better do better than this tomorrow
night, Christiane,' said John. 'You'll be a wreck,
and not a nervous one, either.'

'I do my best,' said Christiane, 'which angels
can't do more than.'

'She does very well,' said Sylvester. 'Besides,
she'll have Glyn to help her.'

At Treleon, Ludovic and Glyn were waiting with
the car, growing more and more impatient every
minute. But after some recrimination they all piled
into the car with some difficulty—particularly as

the back of it also contained shrimping-nets and two large buckets—and set off for Polgith Bay. Glyn was driving.

Polgith was a long narrow bay, quite small, and shallow a long way out. It was dotted with rocks and plenty of weeds, and was an excellent bay for shrimps.

'Space!' said Lois, bouncing out of the car. 'Air! Room to breathe!'

They unloaded the shrimping-gear from the car, and spread out along the shore. Christiane found herself on the far end of the line, and a long way from either of the buckets, so she put all her shrimps in a small rock pool out of reach of the waves. Soon the pool was stiff with shrimps, all swimming round and round, and it would have been grossly over-crowded if she had put in any more, so she sat down on the rocks and watched the others. A short time after, Glyn wandered over to her, carrying a large spider-crab at arm's length.

'Ever seen anything horrible, Rusty?' he asked her.

Christiane took one look at the spider-crab.

'Ugh!' she exclaimed. 'Put it back, Glyn. A long way away from here.'

Glyn dropped it with a splash into the water at his feet, and watched it crawl away. Then he sat down beside Christiane.

It was a beautiful evening, still and calm, with little pinky clouds drifting along against a ground of egg-shell blue, and the sea pinkish-black and smooth, like marble. From the far end of the beach there came the faint murmur of Lois and Sylvester having an argument, but it was not loud enough to disturb the peace, it merely accentuated it.

Christiane broke the silence, saying without meaning to, ' Oh, I wish we could stay here for ever ! '

' What, here ? Or just Cornwall ? '

' Just Cornwall,' said Christiane.

' But you do live here.' Glyn reminded her.

' We're going to London at the end of the summer,' said Christiane.

' But there'll be other summers.'

' There won't.' said Christiane, ' not here. Not for us.' She stared out to sea. blinking back unwelcome tears. It was going to be hateful leaving Cornwall, leaving Lois and John and Glyn, and the sea and the gulls, and the boats and the sand and the rocks, and the faintly antiseptic smell of the seaweed, which was so much a part of the sea. Leaving Treleon, and the small whitewashed cottage which was so much more of a home to them than Stanway had ever been, in spite of all the ancestral associations. in spite of Sir Edward, who was so polite.

' We're going to live in London,' she said. ' In a flat.'

' What a rotten idea ! ' said Glyn. ' Surely you can think of something better than that ? '

' We've tried,' said Christiane, choking on a sob, ' and we can't think of a thing. Oh. I've tried again and again not to cry, because I hate crying, but I'm going to n—now '

' Cry, then,' said Glyn. ' I'll forget about it afterwards.'

Five minutes later Christiane dried her eyes on Glyn's handkerchief, blew her nose with determination, and returned the handkerchief to its owner.

' Better now ? ' he asked.

'Yes, thank you,' said Christiane. 'I'm sorry to be such an idiot, but . . .'

Glyn laid his hand on her arm.

'Tell me about it, Rusty,' he said. 'Surely it's not just leaving here for London that's the trouble?'

Christiane hesitated a moment, but the temptation to tell someone and talk it over with some disinterested party was too great.

'Promise not to tell a soul if I tell you?' she asked. Glyn smiled at her.

'Get it off your chest,' he said. 'What is it?'

So Christiane told him the whole story, leaving nothing out. She told him about Uncle Bob and Stanway, and the sightseers at half a crown a time, and about the first time they had come to the cottage, and how they had liked it on sight, and about the terrific battle she and Sylvester had had with Ludovic to make him give in, and how he had capitulated with a rush after the measles. She told him about the Navy, and about Cousin Lizzie who lived in London and couldn't imagine anyone preferring to bury themselves in the country; and she told him about the fishing-fleet, and about Ludovic wanting—or rather not wanting—to be a bank clerk.

When she had finished Glyn was silent, and she looked at him, trying to guess what he was thinking. He was staring out to sea, his brow slightly wrinkled with thought, twisting his handkerchief absent-mindedly through his fingers.

'Well?' asked Christiane.

'Well!' said Glyn. 'I dunno, I'm sure.' He turned to Christiane. 'Gracious me, Rusty, you do look a mess! Your face is all red and blotchy.'

'I'm not surprised,' said Christiane. 'What can I do about it?'

117

'You're so steeped in sea water already, I don't expect a little more would hurt,' said Glyn. 'Wash in it. You can use my hanky.'

A little later, when she was looking more normal, Christiane suddenly said, 'You won't forget you promised not to tell anyone, will you?'

'On the contrary,' said Glyn, 'I carefully didn't promise anything—don't look like that, Rusty. I'm not going to tell everyone I meet.'

'What are you going to do?' asked Christiane.

'I'm going to start off by having an argument with Ludovic,' said Glyn. 'After that, we'll see. Hullo, the others are shouting at us. We'd better go.'

They scrambled off the rock and went back to the others; but although Christiane remembered her shrimping-net, she left all her shrimps swimming in the pool.

CHAPTER 17

IT was after supper, and Christiane and Sylvester were down at the harbour. The light was nearly gone now, and the anchored fishing-boats were no more than smudges of shadow on a paler shadow. There was no sound but the faint lapping of the waves on the shore, and an occasional burst of laughter from the inn across the road. A bright beam of light was shed on the road from the open inn door, but the twins stood out of its light.

' It's been a lovely day,' said Christiane.

' Mm,' said Sylvester. ' Looking forward to tomorrow, Christiane ? '

' Tomorrow ? ' said Christiane. ' N—no. Not altogether. Part of me is, but another part of me isn't. I wish we didn't have to go.'

' Me too,' said Sylvester. ' It was all right when it was a long way away, but now it's tomorrow it seems a bit silly somehow. But it's the only thing to do. People are so unco-operative.'

' " People " meaning the Colonel and Ludovic, I suppose ? ' said Christiane.

' Who else ? '

There was a long silence, while the twins stared at the dark water and thought their various thoughts. Someone in the inn doorway laughed and called, 'All right, I won't be long. I'll just nip up and tell them. Coming ? '

Someone else mumbled something, and a moment later two people came out of the inn and began walking up the road. Their feet crunched on the loose gravel as they strolled along, talking companionably in low tones. Christiane picked up a small pebble from the top of the wall, and lobbed it into the still water of the harbour. It landed with a faint splash.

' I wish today would last for ever.' she said.

' " Tomorrow is also a day ",' quoted Sylvester. ' Don't be so down in the mouth Chris.'

The two men on the other side of the road stopped, and one of them whistled, a peculiar clear sweet whistle. The twins looked round.

' That you, Rusty ? ' said the man who had whistled.

' Oh. Glyn ! It's you ! ' said Christiane. ' Yes, it's me—us.'

' Just so.' said Glyn as he and his companion crossed the road. ' I was just coming to see you. I—we. that is—this is my brother Mostyn.'

' Oh ! ' said Christiane, taken by surprise. ' I thought you weren't here.'

'And now you can see that I am.' Mostyn laughed. ' I take it these are Armitages and not Treleons. I can't see in the dark.'

' He's not a cat.' explained Glyn. ' These are the Armitages. as you so rightly remark. Rusty, whose real name is Christiane or Christine or Christina or something. and Sylvester, whose name is unforgettable.'

' Real or imaginary ? ' asked Mostyn.

' What ? ' said Glyn.

' Never mind.' said Mostyn.

' Excuse us,' said Glyn. ' We're worse than the Treleons for cross-talk.'

' We've got used to them,' said Sylvester so I expect we'll get used to you too. What were you coming to see us about ? '

'A message from Lois and John,' said Glyn.
'They rang me up because you haven't a telephone.'

'But what did they want?' asked Christiane.

'Mr Swanson has offered an olive-branch,' said
Glyn. 'He's offered to take you all to St Ives
tomorrow.'

'"As I was going to St Ives",' murmured
Sylvester, '"I met a man with seven wives . . ."'

'It's a long way, isn't it?' said Christiane.

'It'll mean getting up at the first crack of dawn,'
said Glyn. 'You'll just about get back in time for
our midnight expedition.'

'Should we go, do you think?' asked Christiane.
'Maybe this is the "getting rid of us" he talked
about—oh!'

'Oh what?'

'I forgot,' said Christiane, confused. 'I mean——

'We are not alone,' said Mostyn. 'What she
means is, she forgot me. You needn't worry—
Christine, is it?—I've been told about it.'

'Oh!' said Christiane. 'And it's Christiane, not
Christine.'

'Call her Rusty and be done with it,' said
Glyn.

'Well, if everyone present is in the plot,' said
Sylvester, 'we'll say it again. Should we go?'

'Lois and John have got to go.' said Glyn.
'Aunt Margaret said so. You may as well go to
keep them company.'

'We can hold the fort here,' said Mostyn,
'between the two of us.'

'You'll be back in time for the tide,' said Glyn.
'Lois said you are to get up early and be round at
their house by eight. I told her you'd probably go,
and I'd ring back if you wouldn't.'

'We may as well,' said Christiane. 'It'll be fun to go to St Ives—even with Mr Thing.'

'Probably be a very instructive day,' said Mostyn; 'how to kid a crook that you don't know he's a crook. You'll have to behave as if butter wouldn't melt in your mouths.'

'Put on a good-little-children act,' said Glyn. 'After all, he doesn't know that Lois burgled his house.'

'Not only Lois!' said Mostyn.

'We ought to be going back to the cottage,' said Sylvester. 'Ludovic will be growing worried. Thanks for giving us the message.'

'Goodnight,' said Glyn, 'and good luck. Keep your eyes peeled for any funny business with that slippery customer.'

'He'll probably kidnap you,' said Mostyn. 'Goodnight.'

'Goodnight,' said the twins. As they walked up the road to the cottage they heard the gravel crunch again, as Glyn and Mostyn went back into the inn.

CHAPTER 18

Lois, John, Christiane and Sylvester were standing on the beach at St Ives, looking with faint distaste at crowds and crowds of people, as thick as ants on the sand.

'Someone once told me that St Ives was the most popular holiday resort in England,' said Lois, 'and I believe them. I didn't at the time, because we'd only just come back from a holiday at Bournemouth.'

'Thank goodness Treleon isn't like this,' said John. 'Well, what are we going to do until we meet Mr Swanson for lunch?'

'Go and look at something,' suggested Sylvester. 'There must be some sort of historic monument around that we could look at.'

'Let's go and look for something,' said Christiane.

They left the beach, with its hordes of holiday-makers, and went back into the town.

'Let's go and see the church,' said Christiane, and so that was where they went since no-one else had any ideas. They saw the famous brass to Otto Trenwith and his wife, which is on the east wall, and with the single exception of Christiane were not particularly interested.

'It's nice,' whispered Lois. 'But boring. Let's look at something else, shall we?'

'Savage,' said Christiane. '*Uneducated* savage.'

The other three left her rapt in admiration of the brass, and went on to look at the carving on the choir stalls, depicting a man in a cocked hat, and a hammer, anvil, bellows and so forth. When they had finished admiring it they found Christiane gazing at the twelve-foot cross outside the south door and they dragged her away to join Mr Swanson, since it was lunch-time. He had left them to themselves all the morning as he had said he had some business to transact.

Mr Swanson at lunch-time was geniality itself, and asked them all about what they had been doing during the morning. Christiane told him that they had been to Porthmeor beach and watched people surfing and playing hop-scotch, and had then visited the church.

'This afternoon,' said Lois, 'we'd like to go to Porthminster beach, which looked a little less crowded, and have a swim.'

'Well, well, you have had a busy morning,' said Mr Swanson, smiling round at them in a way that made Christiane feel about three, and made the others go pink in the face. 'Be back here in time for tea at half past four, and we'll be ready to leave at five.'

'Horrible man!' said Lois when they were outside the inn, and Mr Swanson (needless to say) had left them. 'You wouldn't think he'd pinched our Emeralds, would you?'

'You're not meant to think it,' said John. 'C'mon, you lot. Let's go and have a swim.'

They spent a happy afternoon swimming and lazing on the sand at Porthminster beach (which was very nearly as crowded as the other one but with a more sedate crowd). At a quarter to five they arrived back at the inn, and found that Mr Swanson was nowhere in sight.

'Oh dear!' said Christiane. 'Do you think he's gone away and stranded us?'

'No,' said John; 'his car's still here. I wonder where he is?'

'There's more than one car in the world,' said Lois. 'Maybe someone came and picked him up. I suppose we'd better wait about.'

They waited until almost six o'clock, and then to their relief Mr Swanson came into the inn car-park where they were waiting.

'I'm very sorry,' he said. 'I'm afraid I was detained. Did you have a pleasant afternoon?'

'We had three bathes,' said Lois plaintively, 'and three—no five—sun-bathes. And we're very hungry.' This was not altogether polite of Lois, but, as she said, she *was* hungry and she had been waiting around for a very long time.

'I was about to suggest,' said Mr Swanson with a smile in her direction. 'that since it is so late we may as well have supper here at the inn, because it's too late for tea and you'll be starving by the time you get home.'

'A good idea,' said John. 'But shouldn't we ring up to say we'll be later than we meant? We should have been nearly home by now.'

'That's all right.' said Mr Swanson. 'Lois—you go and ring up your father, and the rest of us will go and order some supper.'

Lois made her telephone-call, telling Aunt Margaret, who answered the phone, that they would be back very late, and would she please tell Ludovic or ask the gardener's boy to tell him; and then she made her way to the dining-room, where the others were waiting for her. She found to her annoyance that she was expected to sit next to Mr Swanson.

Christiane sat on his other side, looking like an early Christian martyr about to be thrown to the lions, and the two boys sat opposite.

Supper, in spite of the uncongenial company, was very pleasant although it lasted for a long long time. Indeed it seemed to the four cousins, who were anxious to get home, that Mr Swanson was being deliberately slow. He made his coffee spin out for nearly half an hour, so that by the time they had left the table and paid the bill it was almost half past seven.

'Later and later and later,' muttered John to Sylvester. 'I don't believe he means us to get back tonight at all.'

'Nor me, either,' said Sylvester. 'But I don't quite see what he means to do with us.'

They climbed into the car again. Mr Swanson invited Sylvester to sit next to him so purposefully that Sylvester dared not refuse in favour of one of the girls. Neither Christiane nor Lois seemed to have any suspicion that they were not intended to get home. although their respective twins were by now sure of it. John sat in the middle at the back, frowning and trying to think what Mr Swanson could possibly intend to do with them.

The car took a long time to start. Mr Swanson excused it by saying that the engine was cold. When it eventually did start it sounded, even to the unmechanical ears of Lois and Christiane, distinctly cranky. Christiane glanced at John, but he was staring ahead of him between the heads of Sylvester and Mr Swanson. Lois was gazing out of the window.

The car limped out of the town.

'I hope she'll get us home,' said Mr Swanson

cheerfully. 'Be a bad thing to be stranded out here at this time of night.'

'Couldn't we call at a garage and find out what's wrong?' asked Sylvester.

'Oh, it's quite all right,' said Mr Swanson. 'Don't start getting worried.'

On the stretch of road between Redruth and St Columb Major the engine cut out dead, and the car stopped at the side of the road. There was only one house in sight, a rather dilapidated-looking cottage, the bare sight of which made one think of ghouls, ghosts, spectres and spooks. Even Christiane and Sylvester, who were so blasé about ghosts, felt a little chilled.

Mr Swanson remained cheerful.

'Lucky there was a house in sight,' he said. 'We might have broken down miles from anywhere. There'll be a telephone, I expect, and I can ring up a garage. Wait here and I'll go and make inquiries.'

He left the car and walked up the road to the cottage.

'Exit the villain,' said Christiane. 'Now what?'

'We wait until he returns,' said John, 'to see what he has to say.'

It was a long time before Mr Swanson came back, and when he eventually did he was looking grave for the first time that afternoon.

'I'm afraid we're in a real hole,' he said. 'No garage will send a man all the way out here tonight, but the woman at the cottage says she'll give us beds, and I've rung your aunt, John and Lois, to tell them what has happened, and they'll tell Mr Armitage.'

'Mr Armitage?' queried Christiane. 'Oh—

Ludovic. But he isn't Mr Armitage, Mr Swanson,'
she added with a dazzling smile; ' he's Sir Ludovic.'
She felt thoroughly snobbish as she spoke, but she
was rewarded by the look of chagrin that appeared
on the enemy's face. Lois gave a subdued chuckle
from the other side of the car.

' Isn't there anything else to do ? ' asked John.
' I mean, it's very hard on the poor lady who has
the cottage, to have five wanderers plonked on her
at such short notice.'

'And we'd like to get home tonight,' said Lois.

' I'm afraid it's impossible,' said Mr Swanson
shortly.

'*I* know,' said Christiane excitedly; ' we could
thumb a lift, and hitch-hike all the way.'

' You will not do anything of the kind,' said
Mr Swanson in a cold voice. ' Come along to the
cottage now.'

There was nothing to do but obey him. John and
Sylvester hung back a bit.

' We'll get a chance later,' whispered John.
'After he's gone to bed we'll slip out and get a lift
—one of us at least. Then we can get word to Glyn
and Mostyn.'

' Is it worth it ? ' asked Sylvester. ' They'll
know what's happened. Ludovic will tell them if
your Aunt Margaret doesn't.'

' 'We'll see what happens,' said John. ' I'd like
to get home. I hate to say it, and never tell Lois or
Christiane I did say it, but I'm rather frightened.'

' What are you two dawdling for ? ' called Lois
from the door of the cottage. ' Come *on* ! '

It was the queerest evening any of them had ever
spent. They sat in the sitting-room of the cottage,
reading out-of-date magazines and listening to Mr

Swanson talking to the rather slatternly woman who owned the place.

At ten o'clock Mr Swanson rose to his feet.

'Well, I'm about ready for bed,' he said. 'You four may as well come as well. We can't stay up late and inconvenience Mrs Smith.'

'Of all the improbable names,' said Sylvester when he and John were in their bedroom, 'Mrs Smith is about the most. Gosh, there is a fug in here of must and dry rot—can we open a window?'

'I don't know if we may,' said John, 'but we are going to. This place is awful. I bet there are bugs,' he added with relish, going over to the window. 'Hullo, it's all wired up.'

'Can't be,' said Sylvester. 'Why should it be?'

'Come and look,' said John. Sylvester crossed the room, but before he reached John there was a tap on the door, and Christiane put her nose round it.

'Can I come in? I say, do your windows open? Ours won't.'

'Nor ours,' said John. 'It's like being in a prison.'

'A prison . . .' said Christiane. 'I say—suppose we are!'

'We'll get out all right,' said John. 'There's two of them and four of us. Anyway, sufficient unto the day is the evil thereof. Leave worrying until tomorrow. Goodnight, Christiane.'

'Goodnight,' Christiane said, and slipped out of the room.

CHAPTER 19

Lois did not sleep at all well. She and Christiane had decided that they did not want to get right into bed, although the beds were made up for them. They suspected fleas and damp sheets, and so they folded back the counterpanes and lay on top of the blankets. At first they fell asleep immediately, they were so tired with the events of the day; but after about an hour and a half Lois woke up again. For a moment she lay looking up at the dark ceiling, wondering what had woken her. Then she decided that she had just woken up naturally, and tried to go to sleep again. but sleep would not come. It was midnight before she went to sleep, and afterwards she could not even swear to it that she had been asleep then.

There was a noise. Only a slight noise, as if someone creeping along the passage outside, trying not to make a sound, had trodden on a creaky board. Lois sat up with caution and peered through the gloom towards the door. A thin line of light appeared under it and as quickly disappeared, and there was another of those stealthy little sounds. She slipped off the bed, and taking care not to wake Christiane, slipped silently across the floor to the door. Cautiously she opened it and peered out. At the far end of the passage where the boys' room was, was the flicker of a torch. Someone tall was standing between her and the light. Lois stepped out into the passage. Faintly to her ears came a rusty scraping sound, like a key being turned in a lock. Someone had locked the door of the boys' room.

'Holy smoke!' said Lois to herself: 'so we *have* been kidnapped!'

The torch flickered again and Lois, quick as an eel, slid into the room next door to her bedroom and found herself in the bathroom. Pressing herself against the wall behind the door, she held her breath—and waited.

Soft footsteps creeping along the passage, the scrape of a key in a rusty lock, and the sound of someone going down the uncarpeted stairs in boots. Lois giggled. It seemed so silly after all that creeping to clump down the stairs in boots!

When she was quite sure that the coast was clear, Lois slipped out of the bathroom and crept over to the stairs. In the hall below she could see a faint light, as if a door stood open and a light was shining through it into the hall. Not choosing to trust herself to the stairs, which might creak and betray her, Lois slid down the banisters and landed with a soft thump, which sounded like the crack of doom to her. However no-one appeared to have heard it, thank goodness, and she was able to creep over to the door from whence the light came. Her heart was bumping uncomfortably as she reached it. There was no sound from inside. She wondered if the room was empty, but while she was still wondering she heard the 'ting' of a telephone being picked up, and someone asking for a number.

'Hullo.' said Mr Swanson's voice after a pause. 'Is that you, Bill? How did it go? You got them? Good. And what about the young baronet. Any trouble there? He saw you? What did you do with him? In the cave? But the tide . . . Quite so. A good idea, Bill. It will look like an accident, and no-one will ever know about the jewels. Bad luck, him coming back like that, though. Any trouble anywhere else? No sign of that young Welshman? Good. I've got the others here quite safe. Mrs Smith will let them out in the morning. I'll slip round in half an hour with the car. It didn't take me a minute to put it right when they were all in bed. Right. 'Bye, Bill.'

There was the sound of footsteps crossing the room. Lois took a wild look round but could see no cover. The front door stood slightly open and offered the only way of escape; she ran silently across to it and slipped out. The car stood just outside. Lois looked at it, wondering. There was no time to wonder for long, however, for Mr Swanson would be coming out of the house at any moment. There was only one source of cover, and that was his car. Lois sped across to it and slipped in the back, lying down on the floor as much out of sight as possible. The door did not shut properly but she dared not slam it. Five minutes later Mr Swanson strode out of the house, climbed into the driving-seat and started the engine. Lois's heart was beating so fast it seemed about to choke her. He couldn't help noticing her, she thought—she felt as conspicuous as the sun in a summer sky.

The car moved off, and the door at the back that Lois had climbed in by began to rattle. Mr Swanson said a bad word, stopped the car and leaned over to shut it. Lois lay on the floor and shut her eyes, praying without realising it that he would not see her. For now there were even more important things than emeralds to worry about. The man Bill had put Ludovic in the cave, and the tide always covered the bottom of the cave when it came up, to a depth of about six inches even at neap tides; it would be higher tonight. If Ludovic was on the floor of the cave unconscious, when the tide came up he would be drowned, and it would look like an accident. Glyn might do something, but where was Glyn? He and Mostyn had not carried out their part that day, apparently. The jewels were taken, and there had been no sign of them. It was dreadful to think of the Emeralds going and no-one there to stop Bill taking them, but it was worse to think that Ludovic should be murdered. There were lots of emeralds in the world, even if there was not all that much money in the Treleon family; but there was only one Ludovic, and he was all that Christiane and Sylvester had. Moreover Lois was fond of Ludovic quite for his own sake. He might be a stick-in-the-mud sometimes, but he was fun for all that. Ludovic drowned . . . . It was unthinkable.

Lois could just see the face of her watch in the dark; it was a quarter past one. Low tide was at two, and the floor of the cave would be covered enough to drown a man lying on his face by three. If only Glyn was around somewhere and she could find him, everything would be all right. He *must* be there.

That journey was a nightmare that Lois never forgot. The fumes from the engine made her feel sick, lying on the floor of the car, and all the time the minutes were creeping past like hours. It was a quarter to two before they reached Treleon, and then Mr Swanson stopped his car outside Treleon House, so that Lois had a long walk in front of her. Moreover, even after the car was stopped, he sat in the driving-seat, apparently waiting, and all the time the hands of Lois's watch were creeping on to two o'clock.

Someone in the darkness whistled softly.

' That you, Bill ? ' called Mr Swanson.

' Everything okay ? ' asked another voice. ' Those kids out of the way ? '

'All safe and sound in bed,' said Mr Swanson with a laugh. 'Any sign of young Lloyd ? '

' Not a whisker. I'm rather surprised. I expected to see him.'

(Was there anything they didn't know ? thought Lois.)

' Got everything safe ? ' asked Mr Swanson.

' Quite safe. I locked up the cottage after me but I left the passage door open, so that it will look like he went down that way and tripped and fell. Miss Penrose is watching; she'll see if anyone by any chance tries to break in, and she'll call the police. We're still waiting for Lloyd to show up.'

' Right. We'll make for Exeter tonight and lie up at the usual. Have you got the doings with you ? '

' Yes.'

Mr Swanson reached over and opened the door.

' Right, jump in and we'll be off.'

Lois stifled a cry of surprise. Surely they weren't going to drive off right now this minute ? Mr Swanson started the engine and the other man closed his door. Lois sat up, taking care not to let her head rise above the level of the seat, and reached up for the handle of her door. As the car started she opened it and dived out into the ditch. The next minute she was on her feet and running down the drive. The car came on behind her; it was close to her—close, closer; they were going to run her down ! She made one leap for her life. Then she was running across the fields towards the cliff.

As she ran she thought: they would not come after her; they would go to the cottage, which was where they would expect her to end up. Obviously they had not thought of the other way in since they had left no guard, and it was only a quarter past two. If she hurried she might still not be too late . . .

By the time she reached the harbour she hardly had breath enough left to push the boat down to the water, and she felt so shaky she could hardly row. The oars would not stay in the rowlocks, and she kept skimming the water with the blades and getting nowhere.

' I *must* be in time, I *must* be in time, I *must* be in time,' she repeated to herself; and whenever she said *must* she dug her oars in and pulled with all her strength.

The hands of her watch crept inexorably round. Half past two. A quarter to three. Now she was opposite the place where the passage should be, and there it was, a yawning black hole with water seeping in and out with a sinister sucking noise. Her breath was coming in painful gasps as she rowed towards it. A moment later the darkness swallowed her up, and she was in the passage.

CHAPTER 20

GLYN and Mostyn had a dull but useful day, weeding the cottage garden under the cold eye of Miss Penrose, who spent the day in her kitchen where she could see them.

'I wish that woman would go away,' remarked Mostyn from the middle of the polyantha-rose bed. Glyn, who was in the cabbage patch, merely grunted in reply. He was in the middle of a fierce battle with some golden rod, which had spread over half the garden and was very old and tough.

'They grow a nice line in stinging-nettles in Cornwall,' he said when he had won the battle.

'Do they?' said Mostyn. 'They grow roses with thorns on too.'

'It *must* be lunch-time,' said Glyn, straightening up. 'We'll eat our sandwiches over here.'

The afternoon was, for Mostyn at least, more peaceful than the morning. They borrowed Ludovic's car, for he had said they could so that Glyn could have driving-lessons, and backed it up and down the road for an hour. Then they parked it outside the cottage, took the engine to pieces and put it together again. After that they cleaned it until everything shone like glass, and then they made it dirty and cleaned it again. By that time it was seven o'clock.

They went separately to the inn for supper, one staying to keep watch, and then played with the lights of Ludovic's unfortunate car for an hour.

'I wonder, could we charge him for the over-haul?' asked Mostyn.

'We could charge him,' said Glyn, 'but I doubt if he'd pay.'

'It's a very good car,' said Mostyn. 'We've found that out for him. I've met many new cars in worse condition.'

'He knew it was a nice car when he bought it,' said Glyn. 'He told me so. What do we do now?'

'Just sit and sit for a bit,' said Mostyn. 'We'll discuss the Highway Code in case Miss Penrose is listening. Have you got that book of questions and answers with you?'

'No,' said Glyn, 'but ask me anything you like. I shan't be able to answer.'

'If you were in a car parked by the side of the road,' said Mostyn, 'and you were going to get out, what is the first thing you should do?'

'Open the door,' said Glyn.

'Ass! See that the brake is on. Then look behind you to see that nothing's coming, and *then* you open the door. Then what?'

'Get out and shut it,' said Glyn. 'I hope I'm mistaken, but I believe Aunt Margaret is coming up the road.'

'Oh help! Where?'

'Behold,' said Glyn, 'I was right.'

Aunt Margaret came panting up to them.

'Oh, there you are! I'm so worried, Martin dear. Lois and John and those other two children have been stranded at some awful place on the road from St Ives—I forgot to ask exactly where—and I do wish you and Glen would go and collect them for me. I don't like to think of them there; they haven't even got their pyjamas, and that awful Swanson man is with them—you know, the cave person.'

' Stranded, are they ? ' said Glyn. ' Well, I never thought he'd do that. Must have stranded himself as well.'

' Well, of course, Glen dear. The car broke down.'

' Well, this car won't,' said Mostyn, opening the door. ' We've had it all to pieces this afternoon, and can vouch for its roadworthiness. Can we give you a lift, Miss Treleon ? '

' Oh, thank you, Martin ! ' Aunt Margaret climbed in the front seat beside Mostyn, and with Glyn in the back they drove Aunt Margaret home, left her and set out for St Ives.

' It would have been very useful if she had asked where they were,' said Glyn. ' The St Ives road is good and long. I say, Mostyn !—we are a pair of idiots ! We left the cottage unguarded.'

' It's all right,' said Mostyn. '*I'm* not an idiot even if you are. Ludovic will be home by now. He was down at the harbour as we passed. I saw him. And we couldn't very well leave one of us behind, with Aunt Margaret there. She's such an old busy-body.'

' That's all right, then,' said Glyn, relieved. ' I felt quite guilty for a moment.'

They drove on in silence at top speed. Mostyn was making the car do fifty, even through built-up areas, because he was in a hurry to collect the twins (both of them) and get back home again. It was at St Columb Major that their fate overtook them. They were speeding through the town when a policeman suddenly appeared and signalled them to stop.

' Oh, something awful, but no strong language ! ' said Mostyn. ' What does he want ? '

'You're going to get your licence endorsed,' prophesied Glyn. 'Well, it's all in the day's work.'

The policeman was in no hurry to open the conversation. He walked round the car, inspecting the L-plates before he spoke.

'The law says,' he began pompously, 'that those learning to drive should have an experienced driver beside them—not in the back seat, sir.'

'But,' said Glyn, 'I'm not an experienced driver.'

'That,' said the policeman, 'makes it worse. And then there's a little matter of speeding in a built-up area.' He turned to Glyn again. 'Experienced or not, you should have a licence.'

'Only a provisional one,' said Glyn. 'I'm the learner. My brother is the experienced driver.'

'Your licence then, sir,' said the policeman, turning to Mostyn. Mostyn did not move.

'I'm sorry,' he said blankly, 'but it's in Wales.'

'Oh, really?' said the policeman, unperturbed. 'Well, I think it would be a good idea if you two young gentlemen came along to the police-station with me.'

'Oh no!' wailed Glyn and Mostyn in unison. 'Surely not.'

'We're in a hurry to get somewhere,' said Mostyn.

'The law is the law,' said the policeman. 'You won't drive any farther tonight. Not until one of you has given me full particulars.'

'We're done, Glyn,' said Mostyn. 'We'd better go quietly, I suppose.'

'You had,' agreed the policeman. 'And don't forget to leave the lights on. . . .'

Ludovic had a very pleasant day fishing, and came back in the evening feeling more cheerful than he had for a long time. He walked up to the cottage humming a little tune to himself under his breath. On entering the hall he found a note which someone had pushed under the door. It read:

Christine and Sylvester will be late back, as Mr Swanson detained in St Ives.
                              Margaret Treleon.

'Mr Swanson?' said Ludovic to himself. 'Someone was telling me some cock-and-bull story about Mr Swanson not so very long ago. *I* know—Christiane. Something about emeralds and the cave . . .'

He screwed the note up and dropped it into the empty hearth, before going into the kitchen. There he lit the fire in the horrific stove and sat down on the edge of the table to wait for it to become hot enough to cook him some supper. While he was waiting he went on thinking about Christiane's cock-and-bull story, and—because he was feeling in an unusually mellow mood, and partly because he was feeling a little guilty about the London business—his thoughts ran something like this:

I suppose I jumped on her rather hard at the time, but those kids aren't going down in the cave for emeralds, diamonds or anything else. But if someone doesn't tell them they're wrong they'll find some way of going down, so I may as well go myself, and perhaps that'll convince them there aren't any emeralds. This stove will take hours to warm up, anyway.

It took him nearly half an hour to unbar the door, and then he had to find a torch. He couldn't find one and in the end had to take the lamp from the kitchen.

The stairs seemed more slippery than before, the broken section more treacherous, and when he reached the bottom—(he'd forgotten he might not be able to get back unaided)—the cave seemed gloomier than ever. He put the lantern down on a convenient rock and began a systematic search behind all the boulders, and in all the nooks and crannies. After a quarter of an hour he found a small box. It was heavy and rattled. It was also locked.

Since the box must either belong to trespassers or be treasure-trove, Ludovic considered himself justified in opening it, and broke it open with the hammer he still had with him from unbarring the door. He lifted the lid and nearly dropped the hammer on his foot.

The box was full of jewels. Necklaces, bracelets, tiaras, brooches and rings, all in a glorious mix-up. Gems of every conceivable hue and all sizes; but the most notable among them was a necklace of emeralds: large, perfectly matched stones, that shimmered and glimmered like green fire in the dancing light from the lantern. Ludovic picked it up almost reverently. It ran through his fingers in a sheen of light, and fell into the palm of his other hand in a heap of colours, all shades of green.

'Good heavens!' said Ludovic. He stood holding it for a long time; and then suddenly he heard a noise on the stairs. Turning, he caught a glimpse of someone coming down, then he slipped on the weeds and fell. His head hit the rock on which the lamp stood, the world exploded in a blaze of light and he knew no more. . . .

CHAPTER 21

BREAKFAST at Mrs Smith's was a gloomy meal.
John and Sylvester were furious with themselves
for not having realised before that Mr Swanson
might leave them stranded, and Christiane was
worried because Lois had disappeared in the night.

' She'll be all right,' said John. ' What annoys
me is—— '

' You've said it before,' said Christiane, ' but
we don't know she'll be all right, anyway. Mr
Swanson might have caught her.'

' She'd have yelled if he had,' said John.

'Anyway, if the Emeralds were in the cave Glyn
will have got them by now,' said Christiane. ' But
I wish Lois . . . ' She stopped speaking and hacked
herself off another slice of bread.

' Pass the margarine, Sylvester,' she said.
Sylvester passed it.

' How are we going to get home ? ' asked John
practically.

' Hitch-hike,' said Sylvester. ' We'll go the
moment we've finished breakfast, and we should
be home by nine.'

' If Mrs Smith doesn't try to stop us,' said John
gloomily.

Mrs Smith, however, seemed only too pleased to
be rid of them, and even went so far as to tell them
that if they walked up the road the bus for St
Columb would pass them and pick them up.

They were lucky in this, because they had hardly
been walking for ten minutes before the bus came
up behind them, and they were able to stop it and

get on. Thereafter by devious means they made their way back to Treleon.

They went at once to the inn. There they found out from one of the serving-maids that the two Mr Lloyds had gone out the night before and had not been seen since.

'Very queer they were acting all day too,' said the girl in a confidential whisper. 'Driving up and down the road, and fiddling about with a car outside Miss Penrose's cottage. I shouldn't be surprised if she's done something wrong and they were detectives come to arrest her. She's disappeared too.'

'Oh, really?' said John, not choosing to deny this rather far-fetched theory.

'I hope they got the Emeralds all right,' said Sylvester. 'Oh dear, what do we do now?'

'Go up to the cottage and have some more breakfast,' said Christiane. 'Aunt Margaret won't be expecting us back yet, and we've still got Lois to find. Leathery egg and bread-and-scrape isn't much of a breakfast, after all.'

They walked up the road to the cottage, thinking about the events of the previous night, and wondering where Lois had got to and what had become of Glyn and Mostyn.

'The door will be locked,' said Christiane. 'We'll have to go round the back. There's a spare key there . . . oh no, Ludovic will be in, of course.'

'If he's not out again,' said Sylvester. 'It's after nine.'

The front door of the cottage was shut and locked.

'Odd,' said Christiane. 'Ludovic can't possibly be still in bed at this hour. We'd better go round the back.'

They went round the back of the house, retrieved the spare key from under a stone and unlocked the back door.

'Now we can find out what happened to Ludovic,' said Christiane, and pushed open the door. She took one step into the kitchen and stopped still.

'Well, I'll be . . . !'

'What?' asked John. He and Sylvester stood looking over her shoulder—and they too were silent at the sight that met their eyes.

The table was spread with the remains of a meal that might have been breakfast or supper, or neither. At one end of it sat Ludovic, sprawled forward on his folded arms, sound asleep. In the armchair by the stove was Lois. Her head was tipped back and her mouth was slightly open. Round her neck shone and sparkled a magnificent emerald necklace, and the kitten was curled up in the crook of her arm.

'Well!' said Sylvester, finding his voice first. 'Would you believe it?'

Christiane let out a long breath.

'And I was thinking how the crooks were going to get away with the Emeralds,' she said. 'But how . . .?'

'Wake them up and ask them,' suggested John.

As he spoke Lois gave a sigh and opened her eyes. The kitten jumped down on to the floor and mewed. Lois sat up.

'What am I doing here?' she asked in a bewildered voice.

'Just what we were wondering,' said John. 'Wake up, twin. It's almost lunch-time!'

'Nonsense!' said Lois with a luxurious yawn. 'It's not eight yet—oh, my watch has stopped.'

'I should say so,' said Christiane. She went over to Ludovic and gently shook him.

'Wake up, lazy! Didn't anyone ever tell you it was bad manners to sleep on the table?'

'What?' Ludovic muttered, and suddenly sat up. 'What's the time?' he demanded.

'All hours,' said Christiane. 'Why—it surely doesn't worry you?'

'Got a phone-call to make,' said Ludovic. 'I'll just slip down to the inn. You might get some breakfast, Christiane.'

He stood up, brushed a hand through his hair, yawned and walked out of the room like a sleep-walker. Lois had quietly gone back to sleep again.

'What a pair!' said John. 'Come on, Sylvester. I'll wash, you wipe, and Chris can get the next meal.'

Ten minutes later Lois woke up again to find the table relaid, and a fearful smell of frying kippers—which was the main cause of her awakening.

'Where's Ludovic?' were her first words.

'He's gone to make a phone call,' said John. 'He'll be back soon. Lois, do tell us, what are you doing here?'

'Where did you get to last night?' asked Christiane. 'I nearly had a fit when I woke this morning and found you weren't there.'

'Mr Swanson locked you in,' said Lois. 'I was in the bathroom.'

'And what happened then?' asked Christiane.

'He didn't see I wasn't in the room,' said Lois, 'and he went downstairs and made a telephone call, and I heard him say to another man called Bill something about having got the jewels and left Ludovic in the cave to drown. So I stowed away

145

in his car, and I went down to the harbour, because I heard them say Miss Penrose was on guard here and I'd never have got in. But they saw me get out of the car, and so they knew I'd heard them, and they tried to run me over but didn't succeed.'

'Full stop,' said John. 'Take a deep breath and we'll have the next instalment.'

Lois giggled.

'You are silly! What happened to Glyn and Mostyn, do you know?'

'Don't side-step the issue,' said John. 'We don't know.'

'Get on with the story,' said Christiane.

'Well,' said Lois, 'I went round to the cave at top speed thinking Ludovic was going to be drowned, but I might just as well not have worried, because when I arrived all out of breath and panting with exertion, he was fishing for the necklace in the water. He slipped and dropped it when Bill came for the rest of the jewels.'

'The *rest* of the jewels?' said three incredulous voices.

'Oh yes,' said Lois, 'there were more than ours there. As a matter of fact . . .' She paused unconsciously to give a more dramatic effect.

'Get on with it,' said Sylvester. ' "As a matter of fact" what?'

'Mr Swanson is the head of a gang of jewel-thieves,' said Lois blandly. 'The police were on his track long before he stole the Emeralds, but they couldn't prove anything. Ludovic rang them up last night after we came here and told them what had happened, and as I heard the thieves were going to Exeter while I was in the car, I expect they're caught by now.'

' Gosh ! ' said John. ' What an anticlimax ! '

' There's just one thing,' said Lois. ' John—I'm afraid the boat is a write-off.'

' Good heavens, why ? '

' Well,' said Lois, ' Ludovic and I were in such a rush last night we came up by the steps and we left the boat there, and the tide will have come up and smashed it to pieces.'

' Daddy *will* be pleased ! ' said John sarcastically. ' Oh well, it was all in a good cause.'

Lois lovingly fingered the Emeralds about her neck.

' He *will* be pleased, yes,' she said. ' Or hadn't you noticed ? '

' Yes,' said John, ' I'd noticed.'

Lois unclasped the necklace and held it in the light for a moment.

' Bill never noticed it wasn't there,' she said with satisfaction, ' the richest haul of them all. He must have seen the box broken open, but the necklace fell into the water and he couldn't see it, so he must have thought Ludovic hadn't touched anything.'

'A colossal bit of luck ! ' said John. ' We've been jolly lucky all along if it comes to that.'

'And all the time we needn't have bothered,' said Lois, ' because the police were hot on the trail.'

' Well, it was good fun while it lasted,' said Sylvester.

' Yes . . . some of it,' said Lois. ' But not last night. That was—horrible.'

Christiane held out her hand. ' May I have a look at the necklace ? ' she asked.

Lois passed it to her. ' Of course.'

There was the sound of voices in the hall, and laughter.

147

'Hey,' said John. 'Who's this?'

'A most harrowing experience,' said somebody. The necklace slipped from Christiane's fingers on to the table-cloth.

'I wonder what happened to them?' she said. The door opened and Ludovic, Mostyn and Glyn came in.

'Good afternoon,' said Glyn. 'I hear everything went wrong. Our fault. Sorry.'

There was a sudden clamour of talk, which ended in an equally sudden silence.

'Did somebody speak?' asked Mostyn.

'What happened to you?' demanded Lois accusingly. 'What were you doing last night?'

'Last night,' said Glyn, 'my brother and I spent in the lock-up at St Columb.'

'Hey—what?' said John.

'He's exaggerating,' said Mostyn. 'We were the honoured guests of Her Majesty the Queen. Speeding, in someone else's car, and without a driving-licence to sport between the pair of us.'

'Of all the foul luck!' exclaimed Christiane sympathetically. 'But what were you speeding for?'

'And what made you desert your posts?' asked John more severely.

'We left, as we thought, Ludovic in charge,' said Mostyn. 'We never guessed the silly ass wouldn't realise, and would disappear at the crucial moment.'

'Thanks!' said Ludovic.

'We were looking for you,' said Glyn. 'Aunt Margaret was worried and sent us to collect you. The fact that she didn't know where you were was as nothing to her.'

'We're out on bail at the moment,' said Mostyn. 'On parole. I expect they'll send us to Dartmoor.'

'Now *he's* exaggerating,' said Glyn. 'We rang up our father this morning and he vouched for our honesty, so Mostyn was—or is going to be—summoned for speeding, and we're all square at the turn.'

'I wish there *had* been a turn,' said Mostyn. 'We might have gone round it and escaped.'

'That was a nice policeman,' said Glyn.

'Those kippers smell about done,' suggested John.

'Help! I'd forgotten all about them,' said Christiane. 'Have you two had breakfast?'

'We have,' said Glyn. 'We had a little bread and water in prison. We'll sit and watch the lions feed.'

'You're welcome,' said Christiane.

The Emeralds were still lying on the table. Mostyn picked them up and held them cupped in his hands.

'And these,' he said, 'were the cause of my being summoned. Just a few coloured beads.'

'Coloured beads!' said Lois indignantly. 'Why, they're worth millions and millions of pounds!'

Mostyn laughed.

'Thought I'd get a rise out of you!' He tossed them carelessly on to the table.

'Was it worth it?' he asked.

'Of course it was,' said Lois. 'Or it will be when Daddy sees them.'

CHAPTER 22

' ONCE upon a time,' said Christiane, ' there was a
good fairy. She must have been the private property
of Bert Beanstalk, because whenever she waved her
wand everything came right.'

' We could do with her,' said Sylvester. ' What
are you talking about, Christiane ? '

' I'm not sure,' said Christiane. ' Sylvester, now
that it's all over—was it really fun ? '

' I suppose so,' said Sylvester, ' but I don't really
like to think of all those people in gaol because of
us. Miss Penrose: she was fairly harmless—even if
she did pretend to be a ghost; but that was our
fault really for not locking the back door, only
no-one ever does in Cornwall—and Mr Swanson— '

' There's no excuse for him,' said Christiane,
' He tried to kill Lois and Ludovic. He was a
horrible man.'

' Yes,' said Sylvester, ' he was. No, the only
one I'm sorry for is Miss Penrose. Poor old bird.'

' She deserved it,' said Christiane. ' Sylvester,
why do people steal ? '

' Not knowing, can't say.' He sat up with a jerk
and brushed the sand out of his hair. ' Lois and
John said they'd meet us here at three,' he said.
' It's now half past. What are they doing ? '

Christiane settled herself more comfortably
against the harbour wall.

' I don't care how long they are. It's such a
heavenly day I don't really feel like rowing.'

' Or sailing ? ' said Sylvester. He glanced along
the shore to where two brand-new gleaming sailing-

dinghies lay on the shingle. 'Funny about that duchess person and her diamonds,' he said. 'And jolly nice of the Colonel to let us use the reward to replace the rowing-boat.'

'With two,' said Christiane. 'It was the insurance company who offered the reward, or he wouldn't have accepted it.'

'I suppose by rights the reward should belong to the police,' said Sylvester.

'Rot,' said Christiane. 'If it hadn't been for Lois those diamonds might never have been found. It was she who heard they were going to Exeter.'

'All's well that ends well, and they *were* found,' said Sylvester. 'Golly, it is hot! Where are those others?'

'I don't know,' said Christiane. She closed her eyes against the glare from the sunlit water. 'I wish we could stay here for ever.'

'You need Bert Beanstalk's good fairy,' teased Sylvester.

'Who needs a good fairy?'

Sylvester and Christiane came abruptly to life and looked up.

'Oh, Ludovic!' said Christiane. 'I never heard you come. Where did you spring from?'

'I suppose you haven't seen Lois and John?' said Sylvester.

'They're at the inn,' said Ludovic. 'I've just come from there.'

He flopped down on the sand in front of them. There was a curious little smile on his face.

'What do they think we've got to do all day?' asked Sylvester. 'Nothing but wait for them?'

'Seemingly,' said Ludovic. 'Actually, though, it's my fault. I told them not to come.'

'Why?' asked Christiane.

'I wanted to talk to you,' said Ludovic.

'What about?' asked Christiane.

'London,' said Ludovic. 'We're not going.'

'What?' cried the twins.

'I talk plain enough, don't I? We're not going.'

'Why not?' asked Sylvester.

'You sound annoyed. Did you want to go?'

'No fear!' said Sylvester.

'Oh, Ludovic, please explain,' said Christiane. 'What are we going to do instead?'

Ludovic answered the question with another.

'Christiane, do you like Mr and Mrs Lloyd?'

'Very much,' said Christiane. 'If I had a mother and father I'd like them to be like them, and I can't say fairer than that.'

'What about you, Sylvester?'

'Say, what is this? Twenty questions?'

'No,' said Ludovic, 'I'm asking for a reason. Do you like them?'

'Yes,' said Sylvester cautiously. 'They're fun. But why?'

'Because,' said Ludovic, 'owing to the fact that Christiane told Glyn about our going to London, Mrs Lloyd has decided that she wants you.'

'Wants us?' said Sylvester blankly.

'Yes.' Ludovic pulled a face at him. 'I can't think why. She's very kindly offered to have you to live with them in Wales—so that I can go to sea and leave you in safe hands. She says they have an enormous house, and it echoes now that Mostyn and Glyn are grown up. And for some reason she has taken a fancy to you two horrors. So has Mr Lloyd.'

'But, Ludovic,' said Christiane, 'she can't, can she? I mean . . .'

'It's a wonderful solution to all our problems,' said Ludovic, 'and *I* don't mind. You can earn your keep helping on their farm.'

'Have they got a farm?' asked Sylvester.

'You couldn't very well help on it if they hadn't,' said Ludovic with a grin. 'Well, what do you say?'

'I don't know,' said Christiane. 'I mean . . . would we pay for our keep, or what?'

'No,' said Ludovic, 'you'd live with them as if they really were your parents, and do everything to help them that you could. The only thing is, I'd pay school fees and pocket-money and holidays and things. Mrs Lloyd wanted to, but I wasn't having any of that.'

'We could come here in the summer,' said Christiane dreamily. 'It sounds like heaven, Ludovic.'

'Then we'll call it settled,' said Ludovic. 'Chris . . .'

'What?'

'I'm sorry. I didn't realise you hated the idea of going to London quite so much.'

'Never mind that,' said Christiane. 'We're not going, and that's that.'

'That, as you so rightly remark, *is* that,' said Ludovic. 'You'd better come up to the inn and say thank you nicely to the Lloyds.'

'"Thank you" sounds so inadequate,' said Christiane, scrambling to her feet. 'As if they'd invited us for a holiday instead of as a permanent fixture. Do you think they really want us, Ludovic?'

'Hard as it is for me to understand, I think they do,' said Ludovic.

'Uncle Bob didn't,' said Christiane. 'Ludovic— it does feel nice to be wanted.'

'Poor little orphan!' said Ludovic laughing. 'C'mon. All aboard for the *Fishing Smack!*'

The three Armitages practically danced along the road to the *Fishing Smack*.

'We'll throw a special celebration feast tonight,' said Christiane, 'and invite everyone. The Lloyds, and Aunt Margaret, and the Colonel, and everyone.'

'What'll you find to feed them on?' asked Ludovic. 'A bit of a crowd, it'll be.'

'Sausages,' said Christiane.

Printed in Great Britain by
Thomas Nelson and Sons Ltd, Edinburgh